"You tryin' to make the fire bigger or tryin' to put it out?"

She jumped at the sudden drawl of Derek's voice coming from behind and whirled to face him. He stood several feet away, his stance casual, hands straddling his denim-clad hips.

"I, um. . .neither." Penny shrugged. As an adult, she'd never told a lie and didn't plan to start. Silence stretched between them while she held the patchwork quilt close and stared back, caught in the act like a barn cat with a fluffy chick dangling from its mouth.

"Okay, here's how it's gonna be," he said at last. "You supply all my meals, starting now, and I'll provide safe escort for you and your girls to Carson City."

Relief made it seem as if a boulder had rolled off her shoulders. "Why, Mr. Burke, that *does* sound like a most practical plan." She directed a hasty smile his way and hurried to fetch a clean tin plate before he could reconsider and withdraw the offer. With the ladle, she dished him up a generous portion of thick stew. "I'm glad you thought of it. 'Tis a grand idea and does work well for the lot of us."

She approached and handed him his dinner. His fingers collided with the tops of hers. Penny gave a short gasp of surprise at the contact. But before she could pull her hands from his warm touch, since he didn't seem in any hurry to move his own, the look in his now dusky blue eyes trapped her, holding her rooted to the ground. Motionless. Her heart, on the other hand, beat out a few swift thumps.

"Truth be told, ma'am," he said, his voice so low it rumbled in his throat, "you had me lassoed with the pie."

PAMELA GRIFFIN lives in Texas and divides her time among family, church activities, and writing. She fully gave her life to the Lord in 1988 after a rebellious young adulthood, and she owes the fact that she's still alive today to an all-loving and forgiving God and a mother who prayed that her wayward daughter would come "home." Pamela's main goal in writing Christian romance is to encourage others through entertaining stories that also heal the wounded spirit. Please visit Pamela at www.pamela-griffin.com.

Books By Pamela Griffin

A Treasure Reborn

Pamela Griffin

Heartsong Presents

To my Lord and Savior, who taught me that sometimes to travel through the wilderness is the only way to know myself and find Him, I dedicate this book.

To many friends I owe thanks—especially to Theo, Therese, Jill, Paige, Ronie, and Mom for being there for me in a pinch and sticking it out with me till the end, as my deadline loomed ever closer. You have my deepest gratitude.

Note from author: Red Cloud's war against the Powder River strongholds, mentioned in chapter seven, actually ended months earlier in November 1868.

A note from the Author:
I love to hear from my readers! You may correspond with me by writing:

Pamela Griffin
Author Relations
PO Box 721
Uhrichsville, OH 44683

ISBN 978-1-60260-005-8

A TREASURE REBORN

All scripture quotations are taken from the King James Version of the Bible.

All of the characters and events in this book are fictitious. Any resemblance to actual persons, living or dead, or to actual events is purely coincidental.

Our mission is to publish and distribute inspirational products offering exceptional value and biblical encouragement to the masses.

PRINTED IN THE U.S.A.

prologue

"You're insane." Derek glared at his brother. His words seethed with rage, though he kept his voice low so no one could overhear. "Either that or you're as ungrateful a cur as I've ever come across. It's bad enough Pa did this to us, but you're telling me I don't deserve one nugget of his legacy? That's downright cruel after all I've done for you, Clay. Or is that just how your mind works these days?"

"How would you know how my mind works these days or any days? You don't know anything about me. You were never around, not since you turned sixteen and took off running. And you weren't there for Ma either. She got worse, and you didn't come home. Even when she sent a letter asking for you."

Derek grimaced at the painful recollection of arriving home four years earlier to his ma's grave. "I told you then that her letter didn't find its way to me till it was too late. A lot like this letter Pa's go-between wrote for him." He crushed the envelope in one hand and paced to the other side of the dusty room, which tried to pass for a hotel parlor but was little more than the size of a horse's stall with a privacy curtain. "I didn't get that letter till after they put him in the ground, either. You can't blame me for what's happened to our family!"

"You're just like him," Clay insisted. "Full of excuses. Always running off. Never around when you're needed. Where you been for the past four years, Derek? Out gallivanting on another adventure through the West, with nary a care to trouble you?"

Clay's childish taunt threatened to make Derek's anger spill over, but he kept a tight lid on his emotions. "Where I've been ain't none of your business, little brother. I made sure you were well taken care of, or did you forget?" Derek stepped closer until he was almost nose to nose with Clay. "It's high time you grew up. You need to stop your whinin' about the past and start behavin' like a man."

Red rushed to Clay's lean face, which still looked too smooth to shave. He took a wild swing at Derek. Before his fist could make contact with Derek's jaw, Derek caught his brother's arm, spun him around, and twisted Clay's fist to his shoulder blades to thwart further attacks. Clay cursed at Derek to let him go, attempting to squirm out of his hold. Derek responded by shoving his brother's slighter form up against the wall, pressing Clay's cheek to the planks, and imprisoning him there with his body.

"Don't ever try that again," he warned.

Clay swore again. "You're a scoundrel, Derek! A no-good snake—just like Pa. You don't deserve any part of that silver mine!"

"Will you just shut up?" Derek rasped the warning low near Clay's ear, his attention darting to the entryway covered by a threadbare blanket to check for unwanted company. "You want the whole of Nevada to hear about Pa's legacy? We're in a mining town, if you'll recall. And there's not one man outside this room who wouldn't like to get his hands on those maps."

Clay muttered something foul under his breath, but to

Derek's relief, he calmed somewhat. A soft clearing of the throat came from the opposite end of the room.

Derek's jaw tensed. He'd forgotten about *her*.

"Maybe if we do as our pa suggested and work together?" the young upstart had the gall to propose.

Derek shot a scathing glance toward the audacious redhead, enough of a warning to keep her quiet. Her cheeks drained of color, and she dropped her focus to her gloves clamped around the drawstrings of her reticule, out of which she'd earlier withdrawn her portion of the treasure map. Everything about the young woman cried indecent, even with the gloves she wore in what he assumed was an attempt to satisfy respectability. Her green silk dress looked like something a lady of the evening might wear and was far out of place in this small mining town, unless she was working in the saloon. After his initial encounter with this supposed sibling he never knew existed and the cantankerous insults he'd hurled her way, Derek had thought Linda would have received the message that she was unwanted and unwelcome, and would have remained mute.

Half sister, my foot!

Derek released Clay with a shove and stomped toward the door.

"Where are you going?" Clay called after him.

"To get to the bottom of this, once and for all."

In less time than it took to saddle his horse, Derek made it to the other end of the small town of Silverton. Passersby on the rutted road took one look at his face and stepped out of his path. For the second time that day, he strode through the door of the claims office.

The squat, elderly clerk behind the desk gave a startled jolt in his chair, his mouth agape when he saw Derek. In three strides, Derek crossed the floor and stood mere inches from the man who withheld the key to his fortune—and only a plank of wood separated them.

Derek noted they were alone and smiled, his jaw tight.

"You again." The clerk made a clear effort to act composed. "I—I told you. I can't answer your questions if I don't know the answers."

"Right. So instead of telling me what you don't know, just tell me what you do know. How about that?" Derek slammed the well-creased envelope onto the desk, causing the stubborn man to give another jump. Good. He meant business and the sooner this go-between his pa had bought realized that, the sooner he could get out of this fool excuse for a town and claim what was rightfully his.

He glared down at the missive, its pithy explanation no more satisfying than the scrap from a treasure map that arrived with it. "A silver mine your father discovered not long before he took sick and died," the note said. "To be split among you and your two siblings, each of whom has received a portion of the same map, per your father's instructions."

Two siblings.

Unthinkable. He'd grown up with only Clay and his ma and had no idea that his philandering pa had married a second wife or had a girl by her. That is, if the marriage proved lawful, and with his no-good excuse for a father, one could never tell.

"Listen," he told the white-whiskered man. "You sent us these notes and had us meet up here, so you might as well tell me exactly where our pa filed his claim. What's the point of sending a map in three pieces? We're all in Silverton now.

Just tell me what we need to know so we can get what's comin' to us."

"I'm sorry to disappoint you, young fella, but as I said before, even if I did know all the facts, I wouldn't violate your father's wishes. Your father was adamant about the order in which matters were to be executed. He explained his requests after he took sick with the cholera, and I don't intend to dishonor the dead. Even if I did claim to know the entirety of the workings that belonged to the mind of Mr. Burke, I couldn't reveal them to you."

Derek narrowed his eyes, and the man gave an anxious chuckle.

"Not meaning to speak ill of the dearly departed, you understand, but he was an odd one, your father. Yet for all his eccentric ways, he was kind; bought me this watch when I expressed my need for one." He fingered the gold disk suspended from a chain.

No doubt a bribe to buy his silence. Such words of goodwill didn't describe his pa, didn't even come close, and not for the first time, Derek wondered if the situation was an ill-brewed sham. As the letter requested, he and his brother had arrived in this isolated town, within days of each other, to learn that their father's body had been laid in a pine box and dropped in the ground weeks before. Or so he'd been told. He had only this man's word that his pa was dead. That, a rough marker noting the gravesite, and three odd letters, each with a third of one map, were all that remained of Michael Aloysius Burke.

"You must know something more you can tell us," Derek insisted.

"If you and your siblings wish to locate the mine, your best recourse is to do what your pa wanted and use the pieces from the treasure map to work together as he specified in the letters. I refuse to tell you anything else. Though as I said before, even I don't know the entirety of the situation. So you can threaten me all you like, but it won't do you any good."

Derek blew out a disgruntled breath, wanting nothing more than to grab the fancy-talking man by the edge of his starched collar and pull his face nearer for a more forceful inquiry. Weariness and hunger made clear thinking difficult. No matter how he searched for a response that would benefit him, a solution refused to present itself. He'd traveled on horseback from the Utah Territory for the better part of a week, ever since a lone rider had hunted him down and given him the letter, and he'd arrived in Silverton only hours before.

The clerk knew more than he was telling; Derek didn't doubt it. But applying force was useless. He'd met up with men less stubborn and sensed this messenger of his father's would never budge. Nor had he ever struck a man, except in defense, and he didn't aim to start now.

With a parting scowl, Derek reclaimed the missive. He stormed from the office, almost pulling the door off its hinges before slamming it behind him, hard enough to shake the thin walls.

Still the anger roiled inside.

As the eldest, that mine should have been his! Derek had spent most of the past decade sacrificing to provide for his family, unlike his pa. And Clay had a lot of nerve arguing that Derek didn't deserve one bit of the profits.

He took off down the road, past countless miners' tents, and again approached the small hotel where the meeting between himself and his estranged brother had been prearranged—and the so-called half sister who likewise had shown up on the hotel doorstep like a greedy kitten in search of a saucer of warm cream. In this case, the cream proved to be an alleged fortune in silver, and he would be hanged before he would let that little minx get her hands on one nugget. Or let his brother lay sole claim to the treasure, for that matter, which Derek supposed Clay had in mind.

He narrowed his eyes as he stood across the street from the ramshackle hotel—no more than canvas walls and roof and a false front of planks hurriedly hammered together, with filthy hides on which to sleep in common rooms shared with other men. Through the door left ajar, he glimpsed a flash of dark red hair and recognized it as belonging to the sly vixen who aimed to steal his inheritance. On the whole, he held women in high regard, but that one was no better than his brother in terms of avarice.

Derek would find the mine without Clay or Linda. And he knew just how to do it.

one

Long before the sun could crown the white-capped mountains beyond Silverton, Derek crept through the room of snoring men with the ease of a wildcat on the prowl. Clay hadn't changed in mannerisms. He still stashed valuables where he slept—in this case beneath the hide he lay on. With stealth, Derek claimed what should have been his.

A twinge of something raw made his heart ache when he glimpsed Clay's face. In the thread of moonlight seeping into the room from beyond closed shutters, his features seemed as smooth and carefree as when he'd been a boy, with no permanent lines of anger or bitterness marring the skin between his brows. Derek pulled himself together and hardened his heart to old memories, shedding all remorse and regrets.

He felt awkward entering the area that concealed the woman who claimed to be his half sister. Hesitant, he pulled back the flap of muslin weighted by stones that sectioned off her room and darted a guilty glance at the sole cot. Of course, she would need a bed and room to herself, being a woman and all. White women in these parts were scarce, but of the few Derek noticed in town, little could be said for their reputations. Linda hadn't flirted with any of the men who'd ogled her from a distance, yet he doubted that greed and deceit were her only shortcomings.

She lay wrapped entirely in a blanket, not a trace of her

brazen hair apparent, a lamp turned down low beside her. Not surprised to see her wasteful use of kerosene, Derek still felt grateful for the dim light to aid him in quietly finding his way around the cramped room. So many fussy bows and ruffles covered her discarded clothing, tossed hither and yon without a care. Loops and bows that could catch his boots and trip him. He hoped she was a sound sleeper.

Derek located her drawstring purse next to her hat on the ground. Within seconds, he located the folded paper and slipped from the room, swamped with relief to leave it, and her, forever behind him.

"You're nothin' but a low-down, lyin' cheat!"

At the angry shout, Derek flinched, sure he'd been caught, and swung around to look.

A few buildings down from the hotel, three rough men stood in the street, arguing outside one of many saloons—still lit up and likely never slumbering. One man swung at another, and Derek took advantage of the distraction to saddle his horse. While the drunks scuffled in the street and still others poured out of the saloon, both joining in the brawl and trying to break it up, Derek rode out of town in the opposite direction. All three portions of the map lay tucked inside his saddlebag, and an unrestrained smile of conquest stretched across his face.

"Sorry, little brother. But this is how it has to be."

Day soon broke over the vast, wild land through which Derek rode. An arid land of rough scrub with its patchwork of remote mountain ranges, canyons, and valleys, it challenged a man's fight for survival. He tried to force down any smattering of guilt for what he'd done, but alone, with no one around for miles to talk to, his thoughts made poor companions. His conscience kept niggling at him as fierce as bedbugs in a straw tick.

His father never abided by any law, man-made or otherwise, but in all the courts in the eastern states, the eldest son usually inherited. He doubted things worked any different here in the West. Maybe his pa hadn't known how the court system operated when he wrote his bizarre excuse for a will; small wonder, rogue that he'd been. Yet through a peculiar twist of fate, Derek had met a talkative attorney in a town he'd ridden through after receiving the letter, and the man confirmed his belief.

Derek tried to ease his discomfort and assured himself that, in a sense, he upheld the law by setting things right. Once he claimed his inheritance, he could be generous—more generous than Clay. Four years earlier when Derek had arrived home and found his ma's grave, he realized after one day with his brother that too much time had passed to mend things between them. So he'd arranged for Clay's care and taken off once again, traveling from town to town and finding work where he could.

Had Derek remained in Silverton, he had no doubt his brother would have done the same: taken the maps in secret and gone off to locate the mine. Derek had just gotten the jump on him. Still, he would see to it that Clay never wanted for anything, not if Derek could help it. Clay was now a young man of twenty, four years his junior, but once Derek became wealthy, he saw no reason to quit his role as provider, despite Clay's resentment. After all, he was his only living kin. And he would supply Linda with enough money to return to wherever she came from, too. He could be generous. . . .

The sun reflected off a thread of silver gleaming in the

distance, what looked like fresh water. Grateful to find a source of such a coveted requirement in a land that didn't provide much, Derek guided his horse toward a small enclosed valley ringed in by low hills of grass, rock, and scrub. A shanty came into view from behind a fringe of sparse trees at the bottom of a rise. Before he could ride past, a gunshot rang out, and a bullet whizzed past his head.

"What the. . . ?"

"Git, you mangy hooligans!" a woman shouted from near the building. He couldn't see anyone in the vicinity. Another shot pursued her command, this time not aimed at him.

From behind a ramshackle structure, hoofbeats pummeled the earth. Derek swung his horse around in an arc to see a pair of riders gallop away. One of the men aimed over his shoulder and shot at the shanty. Not willing to get caught in the crossfire—with no knowledge of who were the outlaws and who were the innocents—Derek scanned the area for cover while making a grab for his gun.

Something sharp struck his hand; he dropped his weapon as he pulled it from his holster. "Ow!" He shook the offended hand, but before he could tell where the missile had originated from, another flew at him fast and hard, striking him in the arm. He slapped his other hand to his stinging shoulder and glanced at the ground. Rocks. Someone hurled small rocks his way. "Of all the crazy. . .who are you? Come out and show yourself!"

Two more stones flew from another direction, landing far off their mark. Derek tried to control his horse; by the way her eyes rolled, he knew she was getting spooked. But he wasn't about to leave his gun behind. At least the bullets from the lone shooter stopped flying, even if the stones kept coming.

Keeping a firm hold on the reins, he slid off his saddle and bent over, stretching his hand out to grab his weapon. Another rock, larger than before, hit him smack in the seat of his pants. He shouted an oath, falling over onto his hands and knees. Smaller stones peppered his back and sides. He held up his hands as if under arrest. "Enough already! I surrender."

The reins slid through his hands while his horse took off as if a lightning bolt had just struck the dirt nearby. Great.

"You just lost me my horse," he yelled.

"Well, maybe if you'd-a just stayed off my land, you'd still have your beast," a woman countered quietly, a hint of Scottish brogue coating her words. She stepped onto the patch of dirt in front of him and kicked his gun well out of reach with the side of her moccasin-clad foot.

He squinted into the glaring sun to size up his attacker. A young woman with thick, dark hair, unbound and blowing about her waist, grimly surveyed him, a gun aimed at his head.

"Well, maybe if you'd-a had a sign saying to keep away, I'd-a done it," he replied calmly, keeping his hands in the air. He didn't trust a woman with a loaded shotgun, especially one as unpredictable as he sensed her to be.

"Everyone with any sense knows to stay off Crawder land, except for low-down thieves and other despicable varmints. Of course, they've got no sense anyhow." She lifted her chin in a lofty manner. "Have you any sense, Mister?"

"After the pounding I got from them rocks, I'd be surprised if I did."

He thought her mouth twitched as if she might smile, but with the sun behind her, it was difficult to tell. She tilted her head as she studied him. "If you're not aimin' to steal my horses or other goods, then exactly what is your business here?"

"Just riding through." The shotgun remained fixed on him, and he added, "I don't mean you any harm. I saw that stream over yonder from about half a mile back and thought I'd rest a spell. I've been riding all day."

For taut seconds neither of them moved; finally, she lowered her weapon. He heard a scuffle of footsteps over dirt and rocks behind him and looked over his shoulder.

Two small girls with dark braids left their hiding places, one from behind a barrel, and the other from the cover of a midsize scraggly bush. Both approached with caution. A slingshot dangled from the hand of the elder, who looked no more than ten, while the younger by at least five years carried a pail full of small rocks. They regarded him, the expressions on their dirty faces wary as if he were an unfamiliar beast of the wild they'd trapped by mistake.

"Your army, I take it?" He looked at the woman. "You trained them well." With the bearer of the shotgun no longer posing a threat, Derek slowly rose to his feet.

"Sometimes a woman alone needs her own fort."

He studied his captor, whose petite figure barely reached his shoulder. Her eyes, on the other hand, were huge. Thickly lashed, they tilted upward slightly at the outside corners and held hints of gold in the brown. Flames of deep red shimmered in her nearly black hair. Her cheekbones were high, her small nose slightly uptilted. The rest of her features, a shade darker than fair, could be called delicate, much like her form. Except for her pert little chin, which proudly jutted out a mile.

She eyed him just as intently, as if still not sure what to make of him, and then turned to the girls. "Olivia, take Christa to the stream to wash up. While you're there, fetch more water for our guest. Our supply is getting low."

"Yes, Mama." The two girls took off running.

"Guest?" Derek cocked an eyebrow. "You always treat company to an onslaught of bullets and rocks?"

She lifted her chin; he hadn't thought she could raise it any higher. "I can be as cordial to a stranger as any hostess, as long as he doesn't cause me or my girls any grief."

He didn't miss her thinly veiled warning. "So, mind telling me what I rode into the middle of? Just what was that all about?"

"Aye, I suppose I owe you the benefit of an explanation." She sighed, her defenses melting as he watched. "Josiah Cribbs and his sons have been giving me grief for some time—miners trying to run me off my land and steal from my supplies at every opportunity. Some weeks ago, they set fire to my barn in the dead of night, but the girls and I were able to put out the flames and save most of it. I suspect they killed my only milk cow three months ago, though I've no proof. One morning, she was right as a trivet; the next cold and stiff, lying on the ground."

"Is there a town nearby?"

"Only Silverton."

He nodded, not surprised. "Has your husband contacted the sheriff?" He hadn't stayed in Silverton long enough to know if the town had anyone to keep the peace but felt he should ask.

"There's no law in these parts. None whatsoever. My husband's been dead since last spring, a year now, and I've kept things running on the place."

"By yourself?" He lifted his brows in doubtful surprise, eyeing her slight form and hands, not much bigger than a child's.

"I'm a lot hardier than I look. And I have my two girls to help me, Mr. . . ?"

Recalling the shotgun to his head and the ambush of stones that struck his body, he couldn't argue her point. With a slight grin, he held out his hand. "The name's Derek. Derek Burke."

She hesitated, no doubt noticing the bruise on his wrist from her daughter's well-aimed missile, before she slipped her dainty hand into his large one and gave it a brisk shake. "Penny Crawder. Why don't you come in out of this hot sun and rest a spell? I imagine you're famished. I have badger stew, still warm on the fire from our noon meal."

He collected his gun from the ground and slipped it inside his holster. "Being as how I lack a horse at this time, I'd be obliged to accept your offer, ma'am."

Her face flushed like a schoolgirl's. "Aye, well, all right then. Come along, Mr. Burke, and I'll dish you up a bowl of that stew."

He followed her into the shanty, hoping he wasn't walking headlong into an even worse predicament.

⸲

Penny put her idle hands to quick use, glad she had plenty left from their meal two hours before. The entire time she sliced the mesquite bread she'd made that morning and brought hunks of it on a plate to the table, she felt the stranger's eyes watching from where he sat.

A clear, strong blue, they reminded her of her da's eyes, though Derek's had the unnerving ability to appear gentle and piercing at the same time. Brown hair, the color of rich, dark syrup, brushed his neck, just touching the tops of his shoulders, and held a bit of curl. His bottom lip was much fuller than his top one, and she noticed how he often pursed them, as though amused at some secret thing. His lean jaw and the skin above his mouth were dark with a day's worth of whiskers. Taller than both her da and her husband, Oliver, had been, Derek filled the chair, seeming to overpower it, his form both trim and strong.

She imagined her visitor had turned many a young woman's head. He appeared in his midtwenties but seemed much more mature, considering the manner in which he'd dealt with their earlier attack. Penny, though no inexperienced schoolgirl at twenty-seven, found his enigmatic presence distracting. He seemed to fill not only the chair but the room as well. Since Derek was also the first man to sup at her table since her husband died, she told herself that must be why she felt so self-conscious. Perhaps it had been a mistake to invite him inside, but she couldn't help feel some remorse for his predicament, though she'd only been protecting her own. Still, while he no longer posed an immediate threat, she kept her shotgun propped within arm's reach against her side of the table. Just in case.

Not sure what to do with her hands, which suddenly seemed awkward and uncertain, she moved to her black potbellied stove, her last gift from Oliver. She grabbed the coffeepot handle with a dishtowel to refill their cups.

"Please, ma'am," Derek said before she could pour. A tiny shiver ran along her spine at the calm, husky timbre of his voice. "Sit down. I have more than enough to satisfy. If I drink any more of that coffee, good as it is, I'll be awake all night."

She poured herself a tad more, set the coffeepot down with care, and wiped her palms down the front of her apron. Running out of methods to keep her hands busy, she at last did as he asked and perched on a chair across from him. She took a sip of her own coffee and folded her hands around the cup. For a prolonged moment, neither spoke as he filled his stomach and murmured appreciative words about her cooking between hungry bites and hasty swallows.

Penny cleared her throat, determined to break the silence before it smothered her. "So, Mr. Burke. You mentioned you were riding through. Where exactly are you headed?"

Did she imagine it, or did his shoulders tense? "Southwest."

She grew alert. "Anywhere near Carson City?"

He took another heaping bite of stew. "Somewhere thereabouts. I think so at any rate."

"You think so?" she repeated, puzzled. "Doesn't the town you're riding to have a name?"

"Nope."

She gave him an incredulous stare. "You don't even know where you're going, do you?"

"I have a good idea where I'm headed."

"Huh." She gave a little scoffing sound. "You sound as if you live the life of a nomadic drifter."

"Well, ma'am, I don't settle down in one place for long, that's a fact. I don't need nothin' to tie me down." His eyes seemed to pierce through to her soul with his message.

"That seems a sorry state of affairs," she replied, all former awkwardness vanishing like dew in the sun. "Putting down no roots means having no friends, no family. No idea of where you're going from day to day, with no legacy to leave behind to your loved ones."

"I didn't say I don't have family." His tone and expression grew dour. "As a matter of fact, I've got a brother."

"I take it there's no love lost between you?"

He looked up from his meal. "Pardon me for saying so, but

are you always this meddlesome?"

She had it coming; still it stung. "I suppose I am." She stood and took his cup to refill it, only just remembering he preferred no more as she again drew near him.

"I didn't mean to hurt your feelings." His voice came quiet. "I'm just not accustomed to talking about mine."

With the slightest smile and nod, Penny replaced his cup. "I should be the one to apologize. I haven't talked with a soul for ages except my girls, and I got carried away."

"I imagine it's difficult, you being out here all alone."

"At times it can be." She reclaimed her chair and looked out the lone window the shanty held, recalling all the troubles that had confronted them this past month alone. "My husband was a good man, but he was no farmer. To my shame, neither am I. The soil is too dry to raise the crop he wanted, despite the stream. And with the constant threat of thieves trying to steal what wee bit I have, 'tis difficult to raise my girls in safety—you're staring again." She turned her head, catching his gaze upon her.

His face tinged red in embarrassment, and he picked up his cup and drained it.

"You're wondering about my origin but are afraid to ask," Penny surmised, accustomed to such curiosity from others during the years she'd lived with her father in a town north of Silverton. "Since I became so personal, 'tis only fair I tell you about myself. My grandmother, my mother's mother, was full-blooded Shoshone. My da said I look like her. She died when I was a wee bairn." She smiled softly, wishing she had known her. "My grandfather was a French-Canadian trapper, my da a Scottish immigrant, his parents both Scots. From him I got what wee bit of accent I have."

"Your parents, they live nearby?"

"No, Mother died when I was a child. Da raised me, teaching me to read and write. He joined her in glory three years ago."

"I'm sorry for your loss, ma'am. But honestly, I was just admiring your bravery at tackling this place on your own."

"I don't know that I'd call it brave. One does what one must to survive." She lifted her brow in smiling doubt. "So, you weren't the least bit curious regarding my heritage?"

He grinned, as if caught. "Well, since you asked, maybe just a mite."

The door flew open, bringing their conversation to an abrupt end. Olivia and Christa, their faces clean and flushed, hurried over the threshold, empty-handed. They came to a quick stop upon seeing Derek, as if suddenly unsure.

"Olivia," Penny said calmly. "Christa. I'm pleased to see my absentminded daughters have found their way home. Did you forget where the shanty was?"

Olivia hung her head in shame.

" 'Tis a good thing I had coffee in the pot and tended our guest. Otherwise, he might have expired from thirst by now."

"I'm sorry, Mama. I forgot." Olivia kneaded her lip with her teeth and turned light brown eyes Derek's way. "I found your horse. In a manner of speaking."

"Where?" He stood to his feet and grabbed his broad-brimmed gray hat from the table.

"Well, um. . ." She fidgeted, sliding the sole of her moccasin along the planks.

"Olivia," Penny prompted. "What have you done?"

"I felt bad that I must've hit his horse with my slingshot and scared it away—I didn't mean to! Honest, I'd never harm any of God's creatures without just cause. I saw it down the valley, drinking at the stream; but I was only trying to make peace with it."

Derek closed his eyes as if fearing the worst, and Penny sighed. "Go on."

"When I got close, it must've gotten scared again. It ran off, north of here. I'm sorry." Her voice trembled with unshed tears.

"Never you mind," Penny said. "Go finish your chores, the both of you. I doubt those miners will be back, not today anyhow."

Once the girls scuttled outside, Penny looked at Derek. "Take one of my horses. If your horse ran north, it couldn't have gone far. The hill that edges that end of the valley rises rather steep, and I wouldn't think a horse would try climbing it."

"Thanks."

"Olivia didn't mean any harm; she was trying to help me."

"I realize that. At any rate, my mare tends to shy easy. She isn't the best tempered beast, but she's all I've got."

"Thank you," she said softly, realizing that was his way of releasing her child from blame.

He settled his hat atop his head. "I best get started so as to get back before the day's gone and leave you in peace."

From the doorway, Penny watched Derek head to the stable, his stride long and sure.

Peace. Strange he should mention such a thing. After her initial suspicions and concerns, he'd put her at ease—more so than she'd felt for some time. His casual and respectful manner invited trust, no matter that he wasn't keen to socialize. Thinking back to their conversation, an idea sprouted to mind. She would dwell on it more, but it just might be the answer for which she'd been praying.

Derek found his bay grazing near the hill the young Widow Crawder had told him about. He approached the animal with slow, careful steps and, with little cajoling, grabbed the reins.

"We've had ourselves quite a day, haven't we, little girl?" The horse gave a slight toss of her head and whinnied as if in agreement. Examining her, he saw no evident damage to her hide from Olivia's stones and no swelling in her legs where one might have struck. He stroked the animal's muzzle before swinging into the saddle and retraced his trek from the Widow Crawder's homestead, leading her mare by its tether.

"You're welcome to share dinner with us," she said once he put her horse back in its stall, unsaddled, and curried it. "Dusk is still hours away, but if you've a mind to consider it, you may as well get a fresh start in the morning. You can bunk down in the barn. There's an empty stall for your horse, too. It's the least I can do after all the trouble we caused."

Derek glanced at the western sky, noting the sun had dropped closer to the horizon. He wouldn't mind sitting down to another of her meals. And he did need a place to bunk for the night. A barn with a roof and hay for a bed would suit much better than the hard ground—at least for one night.

"Thank you, ma'am. I'd be obliged."

After tending to his mare and shucking his bedroll inside the barn, Derek found himself with little else to do and stepped outside. He saw Olivia on the stoop, cutting the tops off a handful of wild onions, and decided to join her. The girl looked up, tilting her head as if uncertain about him, her mannerism much like her mother's.

She opened her mouth to speak, when Christa came running outside. "Mama wants the onions," she blurted then saw Derek. Suddenly shy, she cast her gaze to her fringed and beaded moccasins. He noticed both the girls and their mother wore them, though the rest of their clothes were the type the women and children wore back East.

"Gotta go!" Olivia scurried up from the ground with the pail, disappearing inside.

"Gotta go!" Christa mimicked her sister and giggled, hurrying after her.

Derek smiled and welcomed the solitude. Gazing out over the endless stretch of shrub-covered hills, he mulled over what the upcoming days might bring: with any luck, a mine brimming with silver. As the land turned a deeper shade of green and gold, he wondered if he should offer his help to the Widow Crawder, then decided it best to stay out of her way. He sensed she still wasn't sure about him, despite her invitation to stay the night in the barn, and reckoned if she needed his help, she would ask. Without anything to keep him occupied, Derek paced the area, restless, and looked out over the valley. A nice stretch of grazing land, like a shallow bowl, with low-sloped hills that ringed the outside lay before him. Cattails grew along the little stream. To the east, the granite peaks of the Ruby Mountains touched the sky.

Olivia returned to tell him dinner was on and, relieved, he followed her into the shanty.

During the meal, the girls chattered to one another; Derek gathered the "seen but not heard" rule didn't apply at the Crawder table. Not that he took offense. Their ma acted distant, with a faraway look in her eyes, as if she had a good deal weighing on her mind. He'd never been much of a talker in any case and felt grateful for the respite after her interrogation during the previous meal. He made quick work of her tasty fixings, consisting of badger meat again, but this time roasted with the onions. Once the meal ended, twilight colored the hills a deep, murky blue, and he figured the time had come to turn in.

"Thank you for the meal, ma'am." He stood and donned his hat, heading for the door.

"Wait!" She seemed nervous as she approached, rubbing her hands down the front of her apron. "I'll get you a blanket. The nights still have quite a chill to them." Before he could mention his bedroll, she disappeared behind a hanging patchwork of hides that divided the room and returned, handing him a bundle of cloth.

"Well. . ." He glanced at his boots and tugged on his ear, then looked back into her eyes. Not quite black and not quite brown, in the lamplight they held a tinge of yellow gold and temporarily made him forget what he aimed to say. "I'd best be getting some shut-eye. I'm beholden to ya for the meal and. . .well, everything." Feeling awkward, he tipped his hat and made haste to the stable, sensing her watch him from her doorway.

Once inside the barn, Derek relaxed on his open bedroll with his back against one of the plank walls, the hay beneath a comfortable cushion, and he propped one arm on his upraised knee. He had no idea how much time passed, but his thoughts prevented him from sleep; to his discomfort, the Widow Crawder filled more than her fair share. He'd never met such a woman: In fortitude, she could match any man, though in appearance she seemed as delicate as one of her girls. Truth be told, Derek had never seen such a beauty in all his born days. She had the most riveting eyes. . . .

And why was he sitting here like a dolt thinking about her?

Disgusted with his drifting mind, he doused the flame in the lamp and settled down to get some rest, pulling the blanket over his shoulder. Reclining didn't help matters any as far as sleep went, and soon he found his thoughts taking him back to Silverton. He imagined the thunderstruck looks that must have been on their faces when his brother and Linda awoke that morning to find Derek and the maps missing. The same uneasy guilt that had followed him during his silent exit from the sparse mining town caught up with Derek now. He stared into the dark, trying to push the blame away. He had every right to all that the mine held.

The brush of footsteps in the grasses, slow and careful, alerted him to an intruder. Recalling the Widow Crawder's account of troublesome miners, with the bitter stench of smoke that lingered in the wood of the barn serving as a further reminder, Derek grabbed his gun. With silent ease, he moved to the door and waited

The footsteps came closer.

The door creaked open, letting in a patch of moonlight and a short figure in a broad-brimmed hat and duster coat.

Derek didn't hesitate. Leaping forward, he grabbed the troublemaker, using his body to slam the thief against the wall and pin him there, while pressing one hand hard against his mouth and bringing the muzzle of his gun to the prowler's head. One sudden revelation startled Derek, barreling through his mind: The body against his wasn't firm or solid but yielded soft curves.

The Widow Crawder stared up at him, her eyes huge.

two

Penny's heart thundered against Derek's chest as she gaped up at him; no doubt hard labor produced such solid muscles beneath his shirt. Long strands of hair hung in his face, making him appear wild and dangerous. His riveting eyes, at first murderous, had dulled from shock, though still he didn't budge. With her body pinned against the rough planks, she stood stock-still; even if she'd been free to move, alarm mingled with a strange sense of awareness would have kept her rooted to the ground.

He wrenched his hand from her mouth and retreated. "Woman, what in blazes are you doing here? I could've put a bullet through your fool head!"

Penny worked her sore jaw, rubbing it. "Do you always react with such violence?" She masked her vulnerability with firm words.

"Are you always this foolish?" He shoved his gun back into his holster with unnecessary force. He approached her in the scant patch of moonlight, close, but not as close as before. "I thought you were one of those outlaws who've been robbing you blind! What are you doing skulking about in the dead of night, dressed like a man?"

Affronted, she raised her chin. "You'll recall this is my home, Mr. Burke, and you are my guest. And for your information, these were my husband's things, not that it should matter one whit to you what I wear or why I wear it."

Surprise swept across his face at her quiet attack. She forced herself to calm. Her idiotic pettiness over insignificant matters was of no account; responding with anger defeated the purpose of her visit. In thinking over his action to protect what wasn't his, she couldn't fault him for his rash behavior. Instead, she should thank him.

She cleared her throat, setting her mind on what she would say to steady things between them. "I'm grateful to you for acting in my defense. And you're right—I shouldn't have come. I almost went back to the house, but I heard you moving around and assumed you were awake—and obviously I was right. I must talk with you."

He blew out a long breath, clearly trying to collect himself. "Not to sound disrespectful, ma'am, but couldn't it have waited till morning?" His expression was wary. "It must be nearing midnight."

"Just past eleven. I looked at Oliver's pocket watch before I slipped outside." She didn't add that she'd been drumming up courage to confront him since dinner. At his incredulous stare, she hurried on, "Aye, 'tis late, but I wasn't sure I'd catch you before you left. My husband was accustomed to waking long before daybreak. And I wanted to wait till the girls lay sleeping before coming to tell you I've arrived at a decision, one with which I hope you'll agree."

He narrowed his eyes. "What sort of decision?"

She straightened her shoulders and took a bracing breath. "When you leave here in the morning, I want you to take us with you as far as Carson City."

❧

Derek gaped at the woman, sure she had gone daft. "You can't be serious."

"Oh, but I am." Her steady eyes and the strong lift of her chin did not waver. "I've been hoping to break loose from here for nigh unto six months. My daughters deserve better than to be terrorized by lily-livered cowards who bear me the grudge of not only being a landowner who's a female but also the bearer of Shoshone blood."

"So you aim to just up and leave your home behind?" Derek couldn't grasp such a notion. If he'd owned such a valley, depraved miners or not, he wouldn't consider leaving it.

"What good is it to own a parcel of land if one cannot survive on it? We've managed so far, but I won't be diggin' another grave. As I told you, times have been hard. Especially for my girls."

He shook his head. "That's an awful long distance. Why so far, and what makes you think I'm traveling to Carson City, anyhow? There are a few other towns between here and there."

"You said 'thereabouts' when I asked your direction earlier. My guess is you're out looking for that precious metal which every stranger in these parts is searching for—silver."

Keeping his expression a blank, he hid his shock that she'd read him so well.

She stepped closer, her dark eyes intent on his face. This time, he ignored the same muddled swirl of feelings that had clenched his gut once he realized she was the intruder he'd trapped against the wall.

"When I brought up the glory years of the gold rush, you grew alert—your eyes, they give you away, Mr. Burke. If you aren't out searching for treasure in these hills, then I ask myself, why react so strangely?" He didn't answer, and she continued, "It's been my experience that most drifters find themselves drifting over to Virginia City or Carson City or 'thereabouts,' and my guess is that you're one of them."

"Even if I was," he replied, his tone measured, "I don't aim to saddle myself down with a widow and her two young'uns." The woman added up to danger, as unpredictable as they came. He didn't mind helping a lady in need, but he'd be plumb loco to tackle the risky undertaking of traveling alongside a woman in want. And he felt sure she wanted something in addition to what she asked for. What was more, he was certain he wouldn't like it.

She turned up her palms wide in a beseeching manner. "Please, won't you reconsider? All I desire is safe escort. The girls and I won't get in your way. Once we reach Carson City, you need never see us again."

"And what makes you so sure I'm 'safe'?" he taunted, his voice low, hoping he might discourage her idea by giving her a little scare. "I could very well be the worst desperado you've come across. You might do well to rid yourself of my company."

"You didn't yell at Olivia for what she did to your horse, for what all of us did to you. 'Tis a fact, you were magnanimous about the entire misunderstanding."

"Magnani—what?" He wondered if she'd insulted him with her fancy word, but by the gentle manner in which she smiled, he figured she bore him no ill will.

"You were generous with your forgiveness. But if I didn't think you a man of principles before this, you just proved it to me when you defended my home."

Her soft, earnest praise cut into him like a loose ax head, and he turned away from the plea in her brown eyes that tested his resolve. "Lady, you don't know what you're talking about," he muttered, settling his hands on his hips. "You don't know anything about me."

"I've always prided myself on being a good judge of character." She hesitated. "I don't have much in the way of money, but whatever you deem from my provisions as just payment, it's yours."

"I don't want your money or your things."

"Then what. . . ?"

He spun to face her. "Don't you get it? I'm not taking you to Carson City."

"If it were just me, I wouldn't ask. But my little girls. . ." Her voice wavered. With a mounting sense of horror, he thought she might cry. "They're all I have that's truly important. I'm fair enough with a shotgun but not so foolish as to ignore the risks that traveling alone—and for days on end—could entail."

The tears glistening in her eyes didn't fall, but they near defeated him. He rallied what tattered strength of mind he had remaining. "Try more like weeks. I'm sorry, ma'am. I just can't do it. I won't do it."

Where curtness and intimidation had failed, his quiet words convinced her. Her mouth parted as if to answer; then she gave a little, disbelieving shake of her head and turned on her heel, hurrying out the barn door. It swung shut with a muted *thud*.

Derek passed a restless night with the image of the Widow Crawder's pleading, dark eyes branded on his mind. Long before dawn lit the eastern sky, he saddled his bay mare and rode far from her homestead.

❧

Hours passed with no progress.

Derek glanced up from the map sections he'd smoothed out

over the ground and scowled at the vista of land spread before him. He squinted against the glaring white sun. The rounded hills that stood closest shimmered pale brown speckled with green scrub. Beyond that, the distant mountain range took on the deep color of violets. No matter how far he rode, the land stayed the same.

There must be thousands of rocks and countless more clumps of sagebrush. But no twisted tree emerged, and he hadn't come across any river, either—what he presumed the long, snakelike squiggle from east to west represented. A shaky hand had drawn the symbols, so he only guessed the sketching of three oblong circles, two leaning atop one, was a butte composed of rock. Or maybe three hills closed in together.

Both Derek and Clay learned to read and write from their ma, but Derek figured his pa either hadn't known how to form letters or didn't care to take the effort. Why else wouldn't he print what each symbol stood for? Unless he just wanted to make matters harder for his offspring. Derek wouldn't put such a scheme past the conniver and imagined him rolling with laughter in his grave. If he really were dead. . .could a man that mean really die?

The morning waned. He rode over low hills of scrub, with endless stops and starts, only to circle back, hoping to spot something familiar. A juniper tree? Or maybe the sketch on the map was a tall cactus, like those he'd seen several days southeast of here. Wherever southeast was. With the sun at its highest point, he no longer knew what direction he rode.

"Thanks a lot, Pa."

Muttering in frustration, Derek dismounted. Lack of sleep clouded his judgment. Worse, the water in his canteen was low, though he'd filled it at the creek before leaving the widow's homestead. Now the heat felt close to roasting him like a side of beef.

He snapped off a reasonably straight stick from some prickly underbrush and stuck it upright in dry, level soil. With a rock, Derek marked where the end of the shadow fell. He waited until he felt enough time had passed and marked the dirt again—a method he'd learned to establish east to west in the arid flatlands. He imagined it might work in this high desert country, too. He looked in the direction of the second mark. West. Flicking his hat back from his brow, he felt grateful he'd again found his bearings.

The day passed into early evening. Another stretch of time bore no rewards save one. The plant life became denser, and he spotted some sheep and sighted a small flock of large, white birds flying north; water must be close by. Mounting yet another hill, he looked down into a ravine and noted a reflection that flickered and cut through the gradually sloping hills on either side. Water. He'd found the river at last.

As he drew close, he noticed endless parallel ruts embedded deep in the ground from wagon trains of previous emigrants. He hadn't ridden through here for six years, when Nevada was still a territory, but the river had to be the Humboldt. And that was surely part of the California Trail.

That meant—assuming he'd pieced the map together correctly—somewhere between here and Virginia City on this side of the river, he should find the mine. Question was: Where? And how many miles did the map cover? Ten? Fifty? A hundred? Surely his pa wouldn't have them start their journey from a mining town so far distant. On second thought, it sounded just like something a scoundrel with a spiteful sense of humor might do.

A covered wagon stood alone about a half mile upriver. Having seen no sign of humanity the entire day and curious to know what wayfarers would travel without a wagon train, he rode closer, thinking they might need help. Like as not the owners were stragglers left behind. If the wilderness didn't kill them, the ongoing conflict between the Indians and emigrants posed a threat throughout much of their westward journey and persuaded more than a few less hardy souls to turn around and head back East, which was what he presumed had happened. According to the wealthy railroad tycoons Derek once worked for, the completion of the transcontinental railroad would eliminate perilous travel by wagon train, though Derek sometimes wondered if mounted Indians could outrace a locomotive. He wondered, too, if the Indian Wars would really end, as government officials predicted, once all the natives were forced onto reservations. Or might the battles just take a new turn?

Two small girls with dark braids and wearing moccasins skipped out from behind the wagon. Their giggles carried through the warm, heavy air, as if they thrilled in their adventure.

Derek pulled on the reins, bringing his horse to an abrupt stop. His mouth agape, he recognized Olivia and Christa, then watched their mother walk into view toward the shallow river, a kettle in her hands. None of the Crawder clan had sighted him, and he considered turning his horse around and riding away before they could.

Just as the thought surfaced, the youngest girl whirled around and stared. She ran to her mother and tugged at the back of her skirts.

"Mama, look!" she cried out.

The Widow Crawder shifted her attention from filling her kettle to looking where her daughter pointed. Staring at Derek, the woman rose from her crouch, gripping the handles of the kettle as she hoisted it up with her.

A tense moment passed as neither made a gesture of recognition or greeting. From this distance, maybe she didn't know him. But that didn't make sense; he recognized her.

She turned her back on him and walked away, disappearing to the other side of her wagon. Perplexed, he stared after her a moment, then dismounted and led his horse to the slow-moving water, the width of a creek, first testing it and finding it cold and pure. He knelt at the riverbank and quenched his thirst.

His impulse to turn tail and flee disappeared the moment she walked away, pretending he didn't exist. Now a sense of curious irritation compelled him to make camp. His horse needed rest, and sunset wouldn't be long in coming. That was what he told himself—all truths—but his real reason for choosing to linger was to find out just what that woman was up to.

Last night, she'd fearfully listed the dangers of traveling alone with her small daughters and begged for his help. Now she was out here in the middle of nowhere, with no other escort that he could see. Maybe his first assumption about her had been correct and she really didn't have the sense God gave a mule. To remain on her homestead and fight off attackers had taken daring; he couldn't fault her for her desire to protect what was hers. But maybe a fair share of dim-wittedness also triggered her decisions.

His stomach clenched from hunger, and he pulled from his saddlebag what remained of the dried beef strips. An old fur trader had taught Derek to make the pemmican with dried meat, suet, and berries. But the crimson berries he'd used this time were bitter. He brushed the dust off a brown, leatherlike strip of meat and thought about trying to catch something to roast before day's light faded. The river ran shallow, and through the muddy water, rocks sat along the bed, with no sign of life slithering past, none that he could tell. Nor did he see any small mammals dart through the high grass or brush.

He spread his bedroll on a bare patch of ground. Settling his back and shoulders against a smooth boulder away from any sight of the wagon, he crossed one outstretched leg over the other and stared at the sluggish river. He chomped down into his meal, tearing the tough strip away with his teeth. He supposed he should be grateful for what he had: water and something to put in his stomach, even if the meat had become grainy over the weeks and dull to his taste.

Sensing movement to his left, Derek glanced at the wagon and watched the woman and her girls flutter about their tasks, retrieving items from the back of the wagon. After a few minutes, he shifted onto his side, purposely keeping his back to them. He pulled down the brim of his hat, crossed his arms over his chest, and tucked his hands under his armpits. Forcing his gaze to remain on the horizon, he noted the changes in color as the clouds flamed rose-gold, deep blue and yellow, causing the distant mountain range south to appear almost black. The hairs on the back of his neck bristled. Sensing a trespasser into his solitude, he jerked his head around to look over his shoulder.

Olivia and Christa stood several feet away, staring at him. By the dying light, he noticed their round cheeks and chins stained with bright red. Each of them held a huge slab of some sort of berry pie in their hands.

Berry pie?

Christa raised the thick, messy chunk to her mouth and nibbled on more of the sweet.

Derek licked his lips, watching. "What brings you girls over here?" he asked gruffly.

"Mama said it would be okay if we come and 'pologize to you about scaring your horse yesterday," Olivia said.

"Oh, she did, did she?"

"Uh-huh." Christa gave one huge nod and smiled, revealing rose-colored teeth. "We forgot to after it happened and she said it would be polite and the right thing to do and that we didn' have to wait till after supper 'cause the sun was goin' down and she didn' want us to trip over rocks in the dark or nothin'."

He sighed. "Okay, you said your piece. No harm done; horse is fine. You girls better skedaddle on back to the wagon now."

"Okay." They exchanged looks then glanced at him. "G'night, Mr. Burke!"

The girls took off giggling, but Derek wasn't smiling.

three

On the opposite side of the wagon, shielded from Derek's view, Penny added more bait to her trap, or rather an extra pinch of aromatic herbs to the remainder of rabbit stew. Thanks to Olivia's skill with a slingshot, they wouldn't go hungry; another boon for Penny if she could just do some convincing of that fact to the man bunked inside his bedroll downstream. She had hoped the pie she'd baked the night before when she'd been restless and couldn't sleep would do the trick, but apparently it hadn't. The girls had long ago returned from their undertaking—in the company only of each other.

Penny glanced up. The sky had taken on the color of dry slate, and the air had chilled enough to raise goose pimples on her arms. Knowing she must get some sleep soon if she wanted to be coherent in the morning, she fetched a blanket from the wagon. Dire times called for dire measures, or so her da had taught her.

Olivia and Christa lay inside the wagon, their stomachs filled, both girls exhausted from their first day of travel. The patchwork of hides her da had brought her, which she had stitched together to serve as a privacy curtain for the shanty, now covered her children, keeping them warm. Penny smiled, her heart twisting at the sweet picture of the two girls nestled together, each with an arm around the other, Christa's forehead pressed against Olivia's shoulder.

Her daughters meant everything to her; she would do what she must to ensure they remained safe. Last night, she'd packed the necessities important to start a new life, along with a few precious mementos, leaving behind what she couldn't take. And with the girls' aid this morning, she'd loaded the wagon directly after Derek's departure. But as the day passed without sight of the drifter, she'd worried she might never catch up to him. She'd taken the creek to the river that flowed westward, thinking he would do the same. She'd planned to trail him without his knowledge—at least with the hope of his not discovering them right away, since she knew at some point he likely would—and hoped the sight of him ahead might aid in their safety should any undesirables catch sight of her lone wagon and consider it easy pickings. But after meeting up with him again and not receiving the brunt of a tongue-lashing—in fact, receiving no greeting, good or bad— another idea brewed in her mind.

She grabbed her quilt that covered her trunk and walked toward the kettle steaming over the fire, taking a stand a short distance from it. With steady motions, she waved the quilt beside it, forcing the white smoke that curled up from the black pot to waft eastward. She kept this up for what seemed an eternity but was doubtless only minutes. The spot between her shoulders began to ache.

"You tryin' to make the fire bigger or tryin' to put it out?"

She jumped at the sudden drawl of Derek's voice coming from behind and whirled to face him. He stood several feet away, his stance casual, hands straddling his denim-clad hips.

"I, um. . .neither." Penny shrugged. As an adult, she'd never told a lie and didn't plan to start. Silence stretched between them while she held the patchwork quilt close and stared back, caught in the act like a barn cat with a fluffy chick dangling from its mouth.

"Okay, here's how it's gonna be," he said at last. "You supply all my meals, starting now, and I'll provide safe escort for you and your girls to Carson City."

Relief made it seem as if a boulder had rolled off her shoulders. "Why, Mr. Burke, that *does* sound like a most practical plan." She directed a hasty smile his way and hurried to fetch a clean tin plate before he could reconsider and withdraw the offer. With the ladle, she dished him up a generous portion of thick stew. "I'm glad you thought of it. 'Tis a grand idea and does work well for the lot of us."

She approached and handed him his dinner. His fingers collided with the tops of hers. Penny gave a short gasp of surprise at the contact. But before she could pull her hands from his warm touch, since he didn't seem in any hurry to move his own, the look in his now dusky blue eyes trapped her, holding her rooted to the ground. Motionless. Her heart, on the other hand, beat out a few swift thumps.

"Truth be told, ma'am," he said, his voice so low it rumbled in his throat, "you had me lassoed with the pie." He moved to take the tin of stew, and his mouth flickered at the corners in a lazy grin. "And I sure hope you have some left. Sending your girls out to me when I had nothing but old, dry pemmican, well now, you sure know how to hurt a man. That was pure torture, through and through."

A bit flustered, she didn't know whether to scold him for his roguish and rather familiar behavior or laugh at his dubious plight and discovery of her plan. The flames weren't all that danced in his eyes.

Finding humor in the situation, she gave him an answering

smile. "Well now, Mr. Burke, as a matter of fact, I do have a wee bit of pie I held back in the event I might need it."

"Yeah." He quirked his lips in an amused pucker. "I figured you just might."

Unsure how to respond and still embarrassed that he'd gauged her plan, she moved to the wagon to collect the last two pieces of berry pie.

❧

As Derek led the Crawders along the trail the next day, he shook his head in self-mockery at the proposed arrangement. His mother had once told him a man named Esau gave up his birthright to his brother for a bowl of pottage. He supposed his situation couldn't compare to Esau's story, but the hunger that had gnawed at his belly had led Derek to surrender his privacy and delay his search for the mine, all to provide escort to the scheming Widow Crawder.

The woman was shrewd and as knowledgeable as any man—bold and confident, maybe overly so—in doing what she deemed necessary to steer things her way. His wry disgust with her obvious conniving eased a bit when he recalled her explanation the first night, after he'd caught her skulking near the barn. He couldn't fault the woman for caring for her own and seeing to her girls' welfare. How many years had he done the same for his family, using whatever measure seemed appropriate at the time? Too many to recount. Little good it had done, since Clay didn't understand the meaning of the word gratitude.

Forcing his mind to the more recent past, Derek smirked with the memory of the Widow Crawder's petite form wielding the cumbersome quilt and fanning the fragrant smoke from the stew in the direction of his camp. He'd finally been unable to resist the challenge and silently walked past her wagon, undetected; she'd been so intent on the fire. Moving to stand behind her, he'd watched her actions for some time. Once he spoke to alert her to his presence, he recalled her mortified expression after she'd spun to face him. Odd that his second inclination had been to relieve her mind. His first impulse, and fully what she deserved—to give her a heated earful for her obvious ploy to snare him as her guide as if he were some starving dog in dire need of a bone—he'd pushed aside. One look into those dark eyes swimming with a shamed sort of plea, and he'd decided to put her at ease.

He recalled her joining in his easy laughter and how her eyes sparkled. She really was a handsome woman, her eyes so soft a brown they reminded him of a doe and at times containing flecks of gold that shone in the firelight. Firelight that also brought out the red glowing in her hair...

No, he shouldn't—wouldn't—travel down such trails in his mind. The last thing he wanted was to be saddled with a woman, much less entertain even the idea of courting. The Widow Crawder pegged him right: He was a drifter with every intention of remaining unattached and free—"nomadic" she called it—and that suited him just fine. Derek the Nomad. He turned the name over in his mind, liking the sound of it. Once he claimed his fortune, he would become more of a traveling sheik, like they called those princes in Arabia. Or maybe he'd buy him a fancy outfit somewhere in a pretty little valley. Round him up some cattle and start his own ranch...

"Mr. Burke?"

Torn from his musings, he looked down to see Olivia, who'd come up to walk beside his horse. She'd tied a rope around her waist as a sash, and sticking out from within the hemp rested the slingshot to which he'd been a victim. Nope. Neither the spitfire known as Widow Crawder nor her two daring girls could be considered helpless by any stretch of the imagination. Reckless and foolish, yes—but not helpless.

"Whatcha need, Olivia?"

"You ever been to Carson City?" Her smile came easy. Both girls had been excited to wake near dawn and learn that Derek would be guiding them on their journey.

He looked toward the distant mesa of a wide plain they now traveled. "Can't say that I have."

"Never?" She seemed shocked.

"I'm not exactly from around these parts," he admitted.

"So what makes you think we're going in the right direction? Do you think the city'll be big with lotsa people there? Mama said cities are suppose-ta be big—that's why they call them cities. So how long do you think it'll take to get there?"

He reckoned the inclination to talk about anything and nothing resided in all those of the female persuasion. "The river runs west. Carson City's west. So we can't go wrong by following this river."

She gave him a doubtful glance.

"I rode through Virginia City years ago, so I do recall some things about this area. And I talked to a retired wagon master a few weeks past, saw a map or two." Reminded of his own map, he ended the topic fast; he didn't need her curiosity roused should he slip and make mention of his father's questionable legacy. "The river empties into a sink—that much I know." He glanced to the right at the ribbon of muddy water they followed. "It twists and turns along the way, and we'll have to make some crossings, even travel a spell without water at some cutoffs, but we shouldn't be dry for long." He didn't want to frighten her with mention of the long stretch of desert they would also need to cross.

She was quiet, seeming to concentrate on her moccasins and the path they took before looking up at him again. "So, you a miner like Mama said?"

"No."

"Then how come you're going to Carson City? Isn't that where miners go? And why'd you go to Virginia City? Miners go there, too. Papa told me."

He looked at her upturned face full of questions and chose to give a single answer. "I told your ma I'd help your family get to where she wanted to go, and that's Carson City."

"But why are you in these parts if you're not a miner? Are you a cowboy? You don't look like a cowboy. You ain't got a lasso or spurs, though you do got guns. But near everyone in Silverton has those. I know, 'cause Papa took me with him to town when he went there."

Snooping into others' affairs must have passed from her ma down to her.

"You got the nosy mannerism, too?" He kept his tone mild. He didn't mind young'uns so much, though he hadn't been around many. But he didn't think they were supposed to be so bold and speak their minds. Not from what he recollected of being a youth.

"Nosy mannerism?"

"You like to pry into matters that don't concern you?"

She grinned wide. "I just like hearing the facts, like Mama does and like my grandda did. I miss him. He came to these parts and became a trapper like my great-grandfather. When there was lots of gold found in the streams, years before I was born, Grandda told me he went to look for it, too, but never found anything 'cept a wee bit of gold dust, and he came back 'cause he missed my grandma and Mama. Sometimes at night, I'd hear my papa talkin' to Mama when they thought Christa and me was sleeping, and he talked about looking for silver like my uncle who lives in Carson City. But Papa said he didn't think he'd make a good miner. He said all he wanted was his family, and he didn't plan to go off anywhere and leave them behind like some miners do." Olivia halted her prattle to pluck up some bright yellow wildflowers in a lone bunch near some rocks before running to catch up to his horse again. "So if you're not mining for silver or gold, what'd you come to Nevada for, Mister?"

Derek had hoped she would cease firing questions once she'd been sidetracked by the flowers, and he felt his defenses rise, almost blocking out the pain her cheerful words had caused.

He scowled, pulling his hat farther down over his brow though the sun shone behind them. "Like I told your ma, I'm just passing through."

"To California?"

"Olivia!" Her mother called from the wagon in back of them, likely needing her to clear the path ahead of small rocks or brush so the wagon wheels wouldn't be impeded. The girl whipped around without another word and ran her way.

Derek blew out a thankful breath that the childish interrogation had ended. Between Olivia and her ma, he wasn't sure how much longer he could keep his private matters private. He was determined the Widow Crawder not ferret out the truth of his affairs in trying to stake sole claim to his pa's silver mine. From what he'd experienced of the dogged woman, she entertained no remorse in speaking her mind; nor, apparently, did her girls. He sensed the young widow would soundly condemn his methods, though she obviously possessed a blind eye when it came to her own. And he had no desire to hear her harp her disapproval clear to Carson City.

four

Near sunset, Penny looked across their campfire and watched her silent escort wolf down his stew as if food hadn't passed his lips in days. Thanks to the roots and plants she'd collected through the past year, drying and storing them in her herb box, she prided herself that her aromatic stew was better than palatable, and those herbs that she found fresh made her meals even better.

Derek received a fair portion for his troubles, and she would continue to provide his meals as arranged. Certainly what she offered was better than the pemmican he'd been eating. So the guilt that pricked her conscience made no sense. He'd entered the trade with his eyes open, letting her know she hadn't tricked him one bit. She disapproved of deceit in any form. But lately, her motives were jumbled with confusion about what was truly right or wrong when it came to the safety of her girls.

Derek looked up, catching her gaze on him. Embarrassed, she turned her attention west toward the range of hills and the play of light and shadow as the sun dipped ever lower. It shed deep violet and rose over irregular-shaped rocks, turning them even more intense shades of the earth colors they bore.

"What do you aim on doing once you get to Carson City?" Derek asked, pulling her away from her appreciation of their surroundings. "I reckon a woman as clever as you must have some plan in mind." He handed her his empty tin.

Without asking, Penny took it, ladling him a second helping

of stew. She had learned in the short time they'd supped together that when he set his tin on the ground, he'd had his fill, and when he handed it to her, he required seconds. By the manner in which he regarded her, he clearly read her surprise that he should be the one to ask her a personal question—to be sure, that he should start a conversation at all.

He pursed his lips, and they flickered at the edges in a slow smile. "I imagine it's none of my business," he went on, "and I'm not one to go barging in where I'm unwanted. But since I took on this job as your guide, I can't help but feel a mite responsible for you and your girls. I've never lived in Carson City, but I heard about its workings from others, and it's no decent place for a lady and her two small daughters."

He thought her a lady? She marveled, wondering how long it had been since someone had addressed her as such.

"Living in Carson City is nothing like living in the valley and dealin' with a few ornery miners," he added.

"I'm not going into this blind, Mr. Burke. I'm well aware of the evils involved, perhaps more so than most." Her mother had lived with the stigma "half breed" and the prejudice that came with the name. Her da often told Penny her mother was proud and strong, a convert to Christianity, not allowing the narrow-mindedness of others to sully the person she'd known she was: beloved by God. Like her mother, Penny was determined to face head-on whatever conflicts came her way. Unlike her mother, she felt uncertain she could ever forgive those who brought them and realized she'd failed miserably.

Not all miners were ornery, but she couldn't summon even a morsel of forgiveness toward those men who'd tried to drive her and her children off her land, and in a sense, had succeeded. That only intensified her guilt since her da taught her that God commanded everyone to forgive and that He'd forgiven all crimes men had wrongfully done to His Son. He, too, had been taunted and mocked, looked upon with revulsion. . .then beaten and hung upon a cross to die.

"Olivia mentioned you've got kin there?" Derek broke into her muddled thoughts, which had taken a turn she didn't like.

"My husband's brother. Last I heard, he planned to mine in Carson City. I haven't seen him for more than ten years, and he doesn't know about Oliver. I hope to try to find Ben, though I don't intend seeking his aid."

"Then you do have a plan?"

"Aye." She smoothed the creases of her skirt over her leg in an attempt to remain unruffled. "A good plan. Before my mother died, she taught me to make beaded pouches; I'm certain they would still be in demand and fetch a fine price. I thought to make an arrangement with whoever runs the trading post, to sell them there. In a mining city right off the California Trail, I should bring in good business."

"And just where do you plan on living, if you don't mind my asking? Finding room in a boardinghouse for three new lodgers, two of them children, is bound to be difficult. And a hotel is costly."

She appraised him. "Mr. Burke, for someone who allegedly prefers private matters to stay private and accuses others of bearing a—'nosy mannerism' I believe you called it?—you certainly seem to be living up to the name."

He grinned, one side of his mouth curling up in its usual lazy fashion. "I see your point. But I'm not the least bit comfortable with the idea of dumping you and yours off in Carson City like three lost lambs to fend for yourselves in a den of rabid wolves."

"What are you suggesting?" Her breath caught, and she let it out slowly. Surely, he couldn't be proposing an affiliation of ill repute; he didn't seem the sort of man to take advantage of a lone woman's desire to protect her daughters at all cost. Nor did he seem the type to offer protection through the sanctity of marriage, and she almost laughed at that track off which her mind derailed her.

He looked at her a curious moment, his brow puzzling, clearly noting how she'd choked off a nervous laugh. "I'm suggesting you reconsider and head back home. I'll even provide escort back. We're only a couple days out."

"No."

"I'll admit," he said as though he hadn't heard her low, adamant reply, "you're right handy with a gun and as iron-willed as they come—able to outsmart most any man, I reckon. But not everyone—man or woman—is gonna respect that or take them facts into account. And I'd hate to see any man try to take advantage of a woman. As steadfast and brave as you are, you've no idea what's in store for you in a place like Carson City."

Penny bowed her head, thinking over a reply. She hadn't been mistaken to entrust him with their safety. With each word he spoke, he proved himself an honorable man.

"I appreciate your concern, Mr. Burke, but it isn't your place to decide what's best for my girls. It's mine. And to remain on my husband's homestead would have been unwise. I've struggled with attacks, with near starvation—and with this decision. Why, just the night before we met, I told myself if ever an opportunity arose, I wouldn't ignore the chance. Then you showed up out of the clear blue sky like an answer from the good Lord above. And even though you refused my request at first, my mind was made up that I would leave. Given my life and what's come of it so far, I expect I will face hardship in Carson City, but I'm willing to take that risk. I'm hoping to find at least a few like-minded, godly people and possibly a church or, if not that, a parson to preach God's Word and a better environment for my girls." She thought about the buildings of communal worship her da had told her stood in every town and city in the East and hoped to find such a place in a city of the West.

"A church tucked in among the saloons?" He chuckled at that. "Likely all you'll be finding in the way of preaching is a circuit rider who comes through town every once in a great while," he muttered.

"Then I shall be content with that. A circuit rider is better than nothing at all, and for years, nothing is all we had."

Ill at ease, she looked toward the sputtering flames. She desired to raise her girls to be godly women, but her absence from such women, and men, had caused her own fire to dwindle to embers, the fire for God her da had instilled in her since she'd been old enough to ask questions. Much to her shame, she couldn't remember the last time she'd knelt by her bedside and prayed.

At her sudden twinge of conscience, Penny rose from the ground and whisked the soil from her skirts. "I think all that needed to be said between us has been said. I hope we're agreed that this journey will continue as planned?"

He considered her with steady measure. "I'm not the sort to go back on my word, ma'am."

She couldn't pinpoint the reason, but something about his relaxed manner and the steady way his eyes regarded her made her senses come alert. For an irrational moment, she recalled him pressed flush against her when he'd thought her an intruder, and her face burned with heat. When she'd realized he only meant to protect, she felt both safe and alive, more alive than she had been since Oliver's death. She hadn't been in close proximity to a man for almost a year; surely, the unfamiliarity of that startling moment in the barn with Derek explained why she now relived it while standing across the fire from him.

"Fine," she answered, "that's settled then. I'm turning in. There's more stew if you want to scrape the bottom. I'll clean out the kettle in the morning. You'll tend the fire?"

He nodded, and she strode to her wagon before he could respond. If he chose to do so. She wasn't sticking around to find out.

As she reclined on the wagon boards and pulled the blanket of hides over her, snuggling beside the sleeping Christa in the tight space left, Penny couldn't keep her gaze from wandering to the slit in the canvas, and the view of the lone drifter sitting beside a dying fire.

&

Derek stared into the low flames long after she'd gone. Why should he care so much about the fate of one woman and her two girls? He'd hardly demonstrated the same kindness or concern toward Linda. Even if she was a conniving snake out to steal his inheritance, she was still a woman, the "fairer and more genteel sex," as he'd overheard a sheriff a few days' ride from Silverton put it. He'd had no right to speak to her in the belittling way he'd done. Derek could still remember his sharp, bitter words, along with the cruel names he'd used, and how Linda's face had gone from glowing rosy to chalk white.

Shame gnawed at his gut; he'd never treated a woman, any woman, in the spiteful manner he'd used against Linda. He'd been exhausted, shocked, and angry, but that was no excuse. His ma would have been horrified to hear such vile words spewing from his mouth. He'd reacted like a mad dog at Linda's declaration of kinship. If his ma had been alive, she might have pulled him by the ear to endure a good mouth-swabbing with her lye soap, no matter that he was no longer a boy in knee britches. Now that he'd had a few days to mull over his encounter with Linda—and truth be acknowledged, she did have his pa's piercing gray eyes—he had calmed some. While sharing the company of a young widow who thought him a man of honor, he acknowledged that he'd been nothing more than an uncouth scoundrel.

Once he found the mine and staked his claim, Derek would not only send Linda off on a stagecoach back home, wherever home was, he would also make sure she had enough to care for her needs until she found a husband. She had mentioned she was alone in the world, and Derek supposed he owed her that much—half sister or not. With her attractive face and figure in a land where men far outnumbered women, he didn't imagine her finding a groom would take long. If Derek really was her older brother, as the letter from his pa and her portion of the map seemed to establish, then it was the least he could do for the girl. He sure wouldn't feel right if some calamity befell her on his account.

Recalling his reason for being in this part of Nevada, Derek retrieved his saddlebag and the map. He wanted to look at it by what firelight remained, away from curious eyes, to see if he could recall any of its poorly drawn symbols as resembling anything he'd seen today.

With careful measure, he unfolded all three portions and laid them on the ground before the fire, connecting them into a whole. He smoothed out creases, poring over the faint squiggly line that covered all the pieces, what he assumed to be the river they traveled alongside, and paid particular attention to the symbols on both top and bottom. He recognized nothing, though he'd kept a close eye on the area as they'd traveled—what probably amounted to no more than three miles today, or so it seemed. The widow didn't exactly delay the journey, but she often requested they stop so she could gather cuttings of some plant she'd spotted. In fact, she didn't seem in any real hurry to reach Carson City, though at her homestead she'd implied a need for haste.

A man could never tell what a woman was thinking, Derek reckoned. They still had time before the season shifted full into summer and the heat became unbearable farther west. With that in mind, he hadn't hurried her along when she'd strayed from their purpose. The woman was a fine cook with the few ingredients she had, making her stews come alive, which was what he assumed all the plant cuttings were for. Far be it from him to detract from the makings of a good meal.

He corralled his wandering attention back to the map, again speculating if this was nothing more than his pa's cruel joke, a final slap in the face to the offspring he'd left behind. What if Derek really was wasting his time and efforts on a mine that didn't exist?

A stir at the back of the wagon and the appearance of a small foot stretching out of the wagon's tarpaulin caused him to grab up the pieces of map, clumsily fold them, and stuff them inside his shirt.

The second foot followed, the bearer's white nightdress riding up to her knees before Christa's slight form appeared. Clutching a corn-husk doll in one hand, she slipped to the ground, the hem of her gown falling around her ankles. She turned, caught sight of Derek watching her, and halted in her tracks.

"What are you up to so late at night?" he asked.

"I need to tend to nature's call," she mimicked the words she'd evidently heard spoken by her elders and shifted from foot to foot in clear discomfort.

"Go on then, but not far." He didn't like the idea of having to look for her in the dark if she should trip and fall on the rocks or prickly shrubs; likewise, the threat of night predators always presented a risk outside the safe ring of the campfire. When he saw she headed in a direction opposite to the one he'd thought she would take, toward a cluster of thick undergrowth and rocks, he quietly called out, "Not that way. Go to the other side of the wagon and come right back." He hoped she didn't plan on making this a nighttime ritual.

Christa scurried out of view, as swift as a little white ghost, and Derek let a long-contained breath of relief escape. Had he had his back turned to her, she could have come up behind him and spied the map. Then she might have told her ma.

He would need to be more careful.

The chill air seeped into his bones, and he laid his bedroll close to the fire and slipped inside. But Derek didn't close his eyes until he saw the young'un crawl back inside the wagon and felt sure everyone remained where they were supposed to be.

Even then, he couldn't shake the disquiet that unfurled in his gut at the prospect that hit him: Leading the feisty widow and her two carefree girls across this wilderness and keeping them safe would be a much more difficult task than he'd first supposed.

And by no stretch of the imagination had he assumed it would be easy.

five

The following day went much like the first. Endless clumps of sagebrush hindered travel, and at times, Olivia needed to clear the path of small rocks so the wagon could roll forward. Whenever Penny spotted a familiar plant or flower she needed, she sent Christa ahead to Derek to make a request that they stop.

Not all the vegetation Penny used was for food. Some made good healing teas and poultices, while she used the seeds of other plants as colorful beadwork for her pouches. Of all her tasks, she enjoyed the beadwork most. Images of graceful birds within patterned circles she had stitched with cobalt and yellow seeds onto her own deerskin moccasins, and the girls' footwear she'd also ornamented with similar colors in geometric patterns. Only half a pouch of the precious glass beads for which her father had traded his pelts remained, and she reserved those for a special occasion.

Besides the beadwork, Penny's mother had instructed her in what she, herself, had been taught—that the natives saw the land as one of promise, with each plant and rock significant to daily life. Penny's grandmother, a convert to Christianity, had taught Penny's mother, "Our Father who lives above the clouds created all things for us to survive what my people call tomes, the 'sky motions'; what the Taibonii, the white man, call years. Importance and beauty lies in each cactus; from some we find water for our thirst. . .from each plant, every one with its own purpose. . .from each hill and rock, many which provide cover from our enemies. Even the bones of the creatures of this land serve as tools to aid us. . . ."

Almost able to hear her mother's soft instruction like a faint echo in her head, Penny looked toward a group of high, rocky hills in the distance, an ample area behind which a war party could lie in wait. The sagebrush-covered slopes seemed to radiate the sheen of heat, and at times she thought she saw a flash of light near the top. An arrow? A gun? Or just sunlight hitting the ore in the rocks? She shivered despite the heat and hoped no enemy lurked nearby. . . .

"Mama, please tell me a story," Christa pleaded from the wagon seat beside her. Since she'd woken up that day, Christa had been wan and listless, and Penny had insisted she ride instead of walk.

She thought a moment, putting aside her own discomfort. "What would you like to hear?"

"Tell me about where we come from. I like to hear that."

"First you must have another sip of water."

This time Christa didn't balk at the taste but took from Penny her da's ancient water container made from a buffalo bladder and obeyed without comment.

"My mother's father—your great-grandfather—was a French Canadian trapper who proved himself trustworthy to the Shoshone, my grandmother's people."

"Kimama?"

"Aye, her name was Kimama. My grandfather traded furs with her people for many years before I was born. During the time he lived with the tribe, he and Kimama married."

"He was a peacemaker? That's what Livvie said."

"Olivia is right. He wished only for peace. When the

troubles came, he listened to both sides—the white men and the Shoshone. Once settlers began to move west, many of my grandmother's people feared what would happen to them and their ability to live as they always had. Your grandfather tried to act as a peacemaker, and my da was no different. They met long ago while both were trapping and became friends. Both men understood the concerns of each side and tried to help as long as they lived. Your great-grandfather died in his sleep, six years after my mother, Haiwee."

Penny recalled how, feeling helpless to do more than lend an ear or a nugget of advice when asked, both her da and grandfather had lamented the situation to her mother. Both men had been gifted with the ability to listen and understand. Her mother had also been able to reason and knew peace throughout her life no matter the hardship. But Penny had difficulty seeing the bigger picture, much less understanding the motives of men.

She wiped beads of sweat from her brow with her sleeve and lifted the container to her own lips. Taking a short draft of the warm and brackish river water, she nonetheless felt grateful for the liquid that wet her tongue, then handed the container to her daughter, again ordering her to do the same.

"Ma'am?"

Startled out of hazy reflection, Penny looked away from a distant boulder resembling a skull to the opposite side of the wagon. Their escort had ridden back without her being aware. He studied her from beneath his hat, as though he couldn't quite figure her out. "You feeling all right?"

"Aye, Mr. Burke. You wished to speak with me?" She managed the question with as much dignity as her dust-caked lips could muster. A dry, hot wind had blown most of the afternoon, and she imagined a goodly portion of the high desert's earth stuck to her face as it did to Christa's. Always a stickler for cleanliness, she could scarcely tolerate the thought.

He studied Penny a moment as though doubting her well-being. Despite the ache in her back from the constant pull of the reins for hours on end, she managed to jut her chin up a little higher and square her shoulders, not wanting him to think her weak and in need of special treatment.

"I'm fine," she stated with quiet emphasis.

He offered a short, distant nod, and she wondered if he felt as light in the head as she did. The day had been hotter than others before it.

"All the same, we'll make camp here," he said. "Not that much light left in the sky."

Penny looked west, noting the sun had dipped lower. She figured they had little more than an hour of daylight remaining to cook the sage hen their guide had shot earlier, the feathers of which Olivia now plucked as she sat in the back of the wagon. Between Olivia's ability with the slingshot and Derek's skill with a gun, along with what flour and cornmeal and other staples she'd brought, Penny should keep them all well fed. As for water, if the need arose, they could find that from a barrel cactus, when and if they came upon them. She'd heard tales of how her da and grandfather once traveled southwest, and to quench their thirst, they'd needed to hack the top off one of the spiny plants with a hatchet—a skill learned while her grandfather lived among the Shoshone. She'd never attempted the feat but could direct Derek in doing so.

He'd proven himself strong and quite smart, like her da and grandfather had been. He made an excellent hunter and showed patience with her girls, who could be trying in the best of times. Still, she knew so little about him.

Her mouth flickered at the corners with the recollection of their first meeting, when she and her small pair had gotten the better of Derek Burke and he'd surrendered on his knees with his hands in the air. Given what she now knew of his intellect paired with his skills, she imagined few had been awarded such a sight. Much less been allowed the opportunity to best him.

He watched her, his horse keeping deliberate pace with her wagon. "Something peculiar with what I said?"

"What? Oh no. I agree; this is as fine a place as any. To make camp," she added when he continued to study her.

"You have a queer sort of look on your face. As if you were a mite touched in the head. You sure you're feeling all right?"

Touched in the head? Really! Before he could inquire further and make the situation worse, Penny reined to a stop and called out to the back of the wagon, "Olivia, bring the bird to me so I can get dinner started, then gather some greasewood so Mr. Burke can start a fire. We're making camp here. Mr. Burke?" she challenged lightly as she again turned to him.

He squinted, still indisputably curious, small lines fanning from the corners of his eyes. He tipped his hat. "Ma'am."

Penny tied off the reins and watched their guide dismount from his horse with nimble ease. He wasn't the only one brimming with curiosity.

On hindsight, she'd been foolish to entrust their lives to a near stranger, though she felt her instincts correct and he wasn't a man to be feared. Still, Penny wished to know more about this man who led them, and she no longer felt she could dam the questions from gushing forth.

She took another swig of gritty water from her container, wishing for the sweet, fresh liquid of the stream by her old homestead. Despite the fact she boiled what they drank to prevent sickness, it didn't help the taste. Leaving had been the sensible thing to do, she assured herself as she'd done every day when faced with yet another hardship. Perhaps she felt woozy because she'd allotted herself only small sips all day, giving the greater part to Christa. And Olivia had their other container to drink from. At least she still perspired; her da had warned her that when a man ceased doing that, he could take it as a sign he neared death. They'd passed so many scattered graves of emigrants and bleached bones of livestock along this trail. . . .

"Enough of yer frettin', Penelope MacPhearson! No daughter of mine nor yer dear mither's be a weakling. And you're stronger than most: Ye have the blood of warriors—Scots and Shoshone— coursing through yer veins. Be of a mind to remember that and remember it well!"

She heard her beloved da's stern reprimand wing through her mind as though many years had not elapsed since child-hood, when she'd faced a challenge she'd been fearful to tackle. Her da only called her by her given name, not the cherished nickname he'd coined for her, when angered by her hesitancy to confront something she must, and she'd made certain he didn't often have cause to call her Penelope.

With disgust, she shook herself from gloomy thoughts of the grave and stepped down from the wagon, careful to move slowly so as not to fall. Both she and her daughters would be fine. And tonight, while the cool of the evening settled around them and she felt more lucid, she would put her plan into action and find out what she could about their taciturn guide.

❧

"Mr. Burke, have you an idea of how long it should take us to reach Carson City?"

Puzzled, Derek eyed the young Widow Crawder. At least her skin had taken on a healthier hue and didn't look as faded as before; he'd been half afraid she would keel over once they'd stopped to make camp.

Hadn't they had this conversation before? Or maybe one of her daughters had asked. The three Crawder females did like to talk. Still, he had the oddest feeling by the remote manner in which she posed her question that their timing for reaching Carson City wasn't all that lay in the front of her mind.

"My guess, it should take at least two weeks, maybe more. Assuming we don't come up against any quandaries to set us back." As often as they stopped for plant cuttings, it could take them more like a month!

"Hmm." She gave a vague nod. "Have you ever been out this far west, Mr. Burke? Or farther? Past the Sierra Nevada range and on into California, perhaps?"

Bent over the kettle, she seemed intent on preparing their meal, but he doubted the conversation was as casual as she made it appear. "As a matter of fact, I've been to California."

"Really? Out panning for gold or looking for silver?"

At her mention of the prized metal, he narrowed his eyes, wondering if she'd somehow figured out his secret. "Neither. Most of that's been found, I reckon."

Propping his knee up, he leaned against the tall wagon wheel, the iron rim digging into his shoulder, and nudged the brim of his hat back as he watched her. She continued her task as if she hadn't noticed his unease, and he came to the conclusion that she didn't mean any harm. He supposed she couldn't help it if she was the sort to pry and decided to satisfy a portion of her curiosity. Anything to get her mind off the subject of silver.

"Before coming here, I worked for the railroad. They're laying tracks for expansion through the West. The Union Pacific and Central Pacific are in Utah Territory now, after working from opposite ends of the country to join together. I expect it'll happen any day. I overheard word that each of the leaders plan to take turns driving a golden spike into the final tie." He withheld a chuckle as he recalled the effort it took to lift and swing the sledgehammer to hit the small head of the spike dead center, and wondered if the pampered, well-to-do gentlemen had the strength in them.

"Well, now, that's a pure waste of gold if ever I heard it." She frowned and tasted the stew with a wooden spoon, then threw more of some plant she'd crushed with her hand into the kettle.

"You don't approve of progress?" he guessed.

"My husband wasn't in favor of people losing their homes for progress's sake, and neither am I. We learned from strangers traveling through that settlers were duty bound to leave their homesteads or suffer the consequences—since the surveyors claimed the railroad's best course was to lay track through their land. Supposedly, the railroad tycoons paid them well for their losses, but I don't condone the idea of forcing people off their land. The same thing happened to my grandmother's people, you'll recall, and in a sense to me. Stealing is stealing, plain and simple, and it's just wrong, no matter what government official says otherwise."

He stared, not offering a response to her impassioned words. Her face washed to a bright shade of rose.

"I imagine you're not accustomed to a woman speaking her mind or being knowledgeable about the politics of the day? My husband and father often conversed on civil matters around the dinner table, encouraging me to join in their conversations."

"Truth be told, ma'am, I'm not accustomed to consorting with womenfolk at all. Except, of course, for those women—matrons most of them—who ran boardinghouses or bathhouses in the towns I rode through. And those who fed me. I haven't had a sociable connection with a female in a long time."

"What about your mother? You don't communicate with her?"

Her words, gentle and curious, didn't seem to probe but did hope for an answer. Again he chose to ease her curiosity.

"She died several years back."

"And your father?"

"He's long been gone from my life." His words came out terser than he meant them.

"I see. I didn't mean to intrude."

He doubted her claim, but she didn't see his skepticism. She dished out stew and handed it to him, then ladled out three more servings for her and her girls. "So, tell me, what's it really like being a drifter?"

Olivia and Christa quit sketching pictures in the dirt with rocks and collected their dinner, claiming places on the ground on either side of Derek. He was a bit surprised at how often the two sought a spot near him, sometimes saying nothing at all, other times chock full of chatter, and he felt a mite uneasy for the same reasons. He wasn't accustomed to young'uns or their conversation and often didn't know how to respond. Much like now with their ma.

"What's it like?" he repeated her question. He had no idea where this was heading and wasn't sure he wanted to know.

"Yes, I mean, I've never known a drifter. My da was one for a time, I suppose, till he put down roots and married my mother. But of course, I never knew him in his drifting days, and I've often wondered. My grandmother's people were nomadic, drifting from place to place before they went to settle on the land the U.S. government gave them. But of course, they did so with their families. Never alone."

"Well. . ." Derek pondered a moment on how best to describe his life. "I have the stars for company and soft grass for a bed when I'm not bunked in a hotel in some town, if I'm lucky. I guess you could say the world is my threshold."

"That's really quite poetic," she said with some surprise, as if assuming he'd never held a book in his hands. He may not often have a pretty way with words, but his ma had drilled him in his studies and read to him from her esteemed collection of books during his boyhood days. He figured part of that must have stuck.

"I imagine the days are lonely with no one to share them with," she continued. "I can't imagine living such a life of solitude."

The days had been lonely, but he wouldn't admit it to her. "I never thought much about it. I'm not all that sociable if you'll recall." He ate a good helping of stew.

"So you've said, but I find that hard to believe. You carry on a conversation well when you've the inclination to do so." She paused for a spoonful of her own stew. "Was there no special woman in your past, one who could've changed your mind?"

He managed to swallow what slid down his throat without

choking at her forthright question. Lowering the bowl, he squinted at her, wondering what track her mind had taken this time. "None that appealed enough to make me want to change my course and put down roots—no."

"*Tsk.* That's too bad. I suppose, living the life of a lone drifter, you never reach a stopping point, do you? You just drift about aimlessly throughout the countryside with no true destination in mind."

"I suppose." He took no offense at her soft, probing remark, since to a degree it did ring true.

"And I imagine that, being a drifter, you've had plenty a job besides working for the railroad?"

He pursed his lips and nodded thoughtfully. "I imagine I have."

She gave a soft little grunt, as if frustrated when he offered no further comment. "Aye, well, do you care to be enlightenin' me as to what they were?"

He studied her flushed face, not answering, and she set her empty tin on the ground with a slight bang. He was surprised she'd found time to eat what had been inside.

"Or I suppose we could just sit here and pass the rest of the evening in silence, staring at the wee cactus," she suggested with a wry twist of her lips.

"Yep, we could do that, too."

Derek pursed his lips in a half smile at her stiff remark and decided to play along to see just how far she would take this. Oddly enough, he no longer felt threatened by her endless supply of questions. He had associated with a few women years ago, nothing serious and too long ago to recount well; he'd been a wild young colt visiting the saloon in each town before he'd wised up and quit spending what money he didn't send home on shots of whiskey and cards. But he'd never met a woman like this one, a lady not the least bit intimidated to speak her mind. She captivated him, and he didn't mind looking into those flashing, golden brown eyes of hers as long as she aimed to keep talking—though he wondered if she planned to carry on with this bizarre exchange through nightfall.

The little girls rose to their feet and wandered away, clearly bored with listening to their elders' stilted discussion and in need of other amusement.

"I, for one, prefer conversation, Mr. Burke," Penny said. "I haven't had a good fireside talk with either man or woman in too long to remember."

"Given such circumstances, I'd say that's understandable."

"Is it now? It's understandable. Well then, let's have a go at it, shall we?"

"I figured that's what we were doing."

At his calm, measured words, she lifted her hands in the air. "Och! This is your idea of holding pleasant conversation? I call it more of a cat-and-mouse game you're playing with me, and I'd like this twaddle to cease and to gain solid answers to my questions."

"Why?"

"Why?" She appeared as surprised as he'd felt by her quiet outburst. "You're our guide. I should know more about you."

"Your lack of knowledge regarding my history didn't seem to bother you before when you begged for my help in your barn." The memory of her softness pressed against him when he thought he'd caught a wrongdoer made him lower his gaze to her slight form without thought. He looked up into her eyes again. By the manner in which her lips slightly parted, he wondered if she recalled that moment, too.

"'Pleasant conversation' aside, why don't you tell me the real reason for your curiosity, Mrs. Crawder. Why all the questions?"

"I. . ."

For once, the lady seemed tongue-tied.

"Real reason, indeed! I was desperate that night." She glanced at her lap, smoothing her skirt with her hands. "I've had time to think matters through since then."

"If you're uneasy with my company, I'll go."

"No!"

At her emphatic response, he lifted his eyebrows in surprise.

"I mean. . .that's not what I intended when I said what I did. That you should leave us."

"Then mind tellin' me exactly what you did intend?"

She cleared her throat and fidgeted, plucking at a fold of her skirt. "Only that since we're taking this journey through this wilderness—together—I think it wise if we know more about one another. Don't you?"

Derek held off answering, uncertain what she wanted him to say. He'd told her about his job at the railroad, about his ma, and even answered her question about his pa. That was personal, wasn't it? More than he'd told the men he'd worked side by side with every day. He sensed something other than curiosity settled beneath the exterior of her words, and he wasn't sure he would like it.

"In my travels, I've learned there's an unwritten code pertaining to the West." He kept his eyes and voice steady. "A man doesn't ask questions about his neighbor's past or nose into his affairs or goods—and the two are bound to get along just fine."

"Well then," she said, her chin lifting a notch, her uneasy twiddling coming to a stop. "'Tis a good thing I'm a woman and not a man, so I don't have to abide by such a silly code."

His lips flickered into a smile, and he pursed them to quell it, deciding it best not to air his agreement. For the first time since they'd started this journey, he could admit appreciation for having Penny as his travel companion—and for more than just meals. She could be maddening at times, but her quick wit entertained while her intelligence made for good company. And the pleasurable sight of her womanliness didn't disappoint, either.

Before Derek could form a reply that she just might find tolerable, a terrified scream from one of her girls cut through the descending twilight.

six

Thunderstruck, Penny stared at Derek a split second before knowledge fully hit that one of her girls needed help. She shot up from the ground at the same time he did. His hand went to one of the guns in his holster as they both ran around the wagon and toward the scream, Derek taking the lead.

"Livvie!" Near a piling of small rocks and prickly brush, Penny caught a glimpse of her daughter moving backward. She appeared free of blood and in one piece. "Whatever is the matter?"

"Mama!" Olivia's weak cry offered nothing more as she kept a clumsy and fast pace in retreat. Her gaze never left the ground. Christa stared at Olivia from several feet away, eyes big with fear. Before Penny could grasp the problem, Olivia's heel caught against a rock. She stumbled and fell, then screamed a second time, her apprehensive stare never leaving the pale dirt. For the first time, Penny saw something on the ground dart toward her daughter, who screamed a second time.

"Roll to the side, Olivia!" Derek yelled, bending to grab a fist-size rock. She did, and to Penny's alarm, he threw the rock inches from Olivia, who scuttled backward on her hands and feet. Puffs of dry soil wafted up at the impact.

Olivia scrambled up and ran to Penny, throwing her arms around her and burying her face against her bosom. Instinctively, Penny wrapped her arms around her trembling child. She watched Derek hurry to the spot where the rock landed and kick it aside, then stomp on something with the sole of his boot, grinding it with his heel.

"Did you get stung?" he asked, looking over his shoulder at Olivia.

She shook her head no, tightening her hold around Penny's waist.

"A scorpion," Derek explained to Penny.

Horrified, she broke away from Olivia with a hushed reassurance and moved closer to make certain the creature no longer posed a threat to her children. In the fading light, she noted the brown peril was about the size of her little finger, with its segmented tail now separated from its body, thanks to Derek's boot. The same lightheadedness she'd earlier felt seeped over her at the thought of one of her precious girls sprawled within inches of the vicious dirt dweller. She'd heard a scorpion's sting could be lethal to one so small, or at the very least the victim would be in such excruciating pain they'd wish they were dead. . . .

"Whoa now." Derek's voice came low. His hand went to the other side of her waist and he pulled her close to his side. "Easy there."

He spoke to her as if to an unbroken filly, but she didn't take offense. Penny placed her hand on his chest near his shoulder and worked to regain steadiness in her mind and limbs.

"Olivia's fine," he reassured. "Nothing happened."

She glanced toward Olivia, whom Christa now hugged fiercely.

"I was trying to get some rocks to practice with for my slingshot," Olivia explained as if knowing she'd be asked, her eyes on Penny. "When I turned over that big one, that thing came running from under it toward me. It ran so fast."

"Scorpions can be fast." The words rumbled in Derek's chest, the vibrations they made soothing against Penny, though his message evoked caution. "Best to be more careful from now on. Try not to pick up any rocks larger than a pebble."

"I will," Olivia promised. "Thank you, Mr. Burke."

"Glad to help."

"Aye, thank you." Penny stepped away from Derek, confused by her heart's strange reaction, skipping beats, and the way her breath caught in her throat. She felt even more perplexed that she missed his warm strength and wanted to retrace that step back into his arms to be held by him a moment longer. There she'd felt safe, an emotion she hadn't felt in a long while. To cover her confusion, she took charge.

"Girls, get on back to the wagon and ready yourselves for bed," she ordered, thankful to find her voice again. "The scare is over."

"Yes, Mama." Both girls ran for the wagon.

"You all right?" Derek asked when Penny remained fixed. She sensed his gaze intent on her face, however she couldn't look at him, not with her emotions still in a whirl.

" 'Twas a momentary spell. Rather inane when I think of the many hardships we've faced. I've encountered scorpions before. And to react so strongly at such an occurrence when all worked out well in the end—well, that was foolish. I've never come so close to swooning in my life."

"Don't take on so," he soothed. "I expect every man or woman has that staggering moment when they come up against the unexpected and it knocks their feet right out from under them. I imagine the heat today didn't help matters, either. It takes time to get accustomed to traveling in it. Have you been drinking water?"

"Aye." She wondered if he'd forgotten this was her home. True, four days away and not as barren as the land through which they now traveled, and she'd possessed a roof to give her shelter from the unforgiving sun, though it had seldom been as hot. Nonetheless, it was a land with which she was familiar.

The rest of the evening passed without occasion. After she'd cleaned up from supper and stored the utensils, she returned the small crate to the wagon. Her gaze went past her sleeping children to the trunk that took up a third of the wagon bed; it had taken all three of them to load it, and they'd had to empty it beforehand. Penny thought a moment, then grabbed the lantern hanging outside the wagon, climbed within the shielding canvas, and pulled up the heavy lid.

With care, she lifted a fold of her mother's wedding dress from the trunk, admiring the intricate beadwork that both her grandmother and mother had sewn at the neck and hem. Symbols that told her mother's story and of meeting Penny's father, symbols of happiness for their future. She pulled the dress all the way out, and a fall of the soft, tanned deerskin poured down in light brown folds to her lap. Her fingertips rested over one rectangle of many in the cobalt, green, and white seed and stone beads, and her mind wandered as it had often done of late.

A long time had elapsed since she'd felt or behaved like a woman with a woman's soft qualities; she wondered if any such traits still existed inside her. For what seemed endless months, she had needed to assume the fierce, protective, and fighting characteristics of a man and taken on a man's job to protect what was hers. In the process, she felt her womanliness had dissolved. Had her da or husband been alive, she doubted they would even recognize her. She'd been astounded when Derek referred to her as a lady on their first day of traveling together.

Penny thought about their quiet guide and the odd desire she experienced to be near him. She had long hoped for a God-fearing, faithful companion, a hard worker, someone to become a good father to her girls, and had made the request for months in prayer. She'd loved her husband, but time dulled the pain of losing him and helped her to let go. She felt prepared not only to accept the notion of marrying again but also to picture her future with another man. The more she learned of Derek Burke—however difficult the task to piece together such information—the less she believed any man other than Derek could take the place of Oliver.

She'd heard tales from her father of God-fearing men and women who married for convenience's sake, some barely knowing the other. Some men sent for brides from the East, sight unseen. With that knowledge, she didn't discount the possibility of a union despite their scant time together. But Derek made it clear he planned to remain a drifter, more or less stating flat out that he didn't have it in his mind to settle down with any woman. Could she change his heart to reconsider the idea? Did she truly wish to? Or were such ideas nonsense and too soon in their acquaintance to broach or even ponder?

"What's that you're holding, Mama?" Olivia questioned.

Surprised, Penny looked her daughter's way. "I thought you were asleep."

Olivia's tousled, dark braids swept her nightdress, one falling over her shoulder to the small of her back as she rose to sit in the cramped wagon. "The light got in my eyes when they was shut, but I couldn't sleep anyhow."

"Were shut." Recalling her daughter's earlier scare, Penny wasn't surprised. She noticed Christa's face bore a slight smile as she slumbered like an angel curled up beside Olivia and felt grateful that one of her children invited sweet dreams. Her gaze returned to the velvety cloth in her lap. "This was your grandmother's dress. She wore it for her wedding and other special occasions."

"Did you wear it when you married Papa?"

"No, I made another." Penny's remark came distant, her mind still wrapped up in Derek.

"Why didn't you wear this one? It's so pretty."

"Aye." She couldn't explain to her daughter that Oliver's parents had never accepted her because of her heritage. Out of respect to Oliver, she'd foregone wearing to the ceremony anything native that might provoke disapproval from them, but often since then, she'd regretted her decision.

"You going to wear it tomorrow?"

"What?" Penny looked at her eldest daughter in surprise.

"You should wear it, Mama. It would look nice on you."

"This isn't a dress one would wear to travel through the wilds."

"Why not?"

Why not, indeed!

"Mr. Burke might think it's pretty, too."

Christa giggled, and Penny sent a sharp glance her way. Her youngest child had one eye opened and quickly shut it.

"So, Christabel Louise, are you playing possum, too?" Penny asked, deciding to ignore Olivia's last comment.

"Playing possum?" Christa pushed herself up to sit beside her sister.

"What your grandda said to me when I was your age. It means pretending to sleep."

"I did try—honest." She covered her mouth with her hand to smother another giggle.

"Of course you did," Penny agreed with mock sternness, doubting it. She imagined both girls had been whispering together as they often did at night. Yet this night, she would not scold. This night felt oddly different, as if a strange weight of import had come to rest on her shoulders. Catching sight of the sacred book in her trunk, she thought she understood in part and resolved to resume a lost tradition in full.

She folded the dress, setting it back in its sheltered place, and pulled out the book. "Do you girls know what this is?"

Christa shook her head no, and Olivia drew closer to peer at the leather-bound cover.

"You don't recall when your papa would read to you from the Holy Bible?"

"I remember," Olivia answered quietly.

"Aye, you did love to sit at his knee." Penny sighed with bittersweet fondness at the mental image her words evoked. "This belonged to my mother. My da sent for it from back East during a trip to town. He taught my mother to read from these pages just as a parson's wife taught him from one similar when he was newly come from Edinburgh to Boston as a youth. He stayed with the parson and his wife for a time. Not many people then or now receive the privilege of such instruction—to read and write. And sadly others, though they can read, never learn the words from this book. My parents were two of the fortunate ones, and what they taught me,

I now teach you."

The girls' eyes widened as Penny spoke, and they each gave a solemn nod.

She opened the cover and caressed the thin, onionskin-like page with tender remembrance. A dried flower stem stuck out from between the bottom of some pages, and she turned to that section of the New Testament. She couldn't recall having seen the stem before or how it got there, and wondered if it had been her mother's. "I want to renew the tradition of reading from this book each night. I think it would be pleasing to God, and we should strive to please Him in all that we do. We want to start out our new life as it should be." *And should have been all along.*

Penny had attempted to carry on with the readings after Oliver died, and for a while, she had succeeded. But the cares of the world weighed upon her, until one evening she forgot to retrieve the Bible from its place in her trunk. With the difficulties that continued to beset her daily, forgetting had become easier with the passage of time.

Forgive me, Father, for disobeying Your Word and not keeping up the custom of sharing with my girls what lies within Your Holy Book.

After issuing her silent prayer, she drew the kerosene lamp close. It would probably be wisest to conserve oil and use the dawn's light to read the tiny print, and after this night, she planned to do just that. But now that she'd retrieved the family Bible from her trunk and the pages lay open, she didn't wish to put it off any longer. A long-fermented seed of eagerness sprouted within her heart to again turn its pages and look upon the stirring words. She instructed her girls to lie down but to keep their eyes open.

"This isn't a bedtime tale," she explained while they did as they were told. "Not one like your grandda told you, before he went to live in glory. There are accounts of adventure within, 'tis true, much like your grandda's stories were—but this is the Almighty God's Word and His message. It's important you not only hear these words but that you act on them so your life will be blessed."

"Yes, Mama," her daughters said one after the other. Their brown eyes big and full of curious anticipation, they again pulled the quilt of hides over them as they prepared to listen.

In a low, soothing voice, Penny read the page on which the dried flower marker rested, figuring it as good a place as any to start. She read to them parables that Jesus Christ told. But when she reached the Lord's instruction to forgive a man seventy times seven, she grew troubled and ended the reading.

The girls' eyes were heavy-lidded as she smoothed their hair and kissed them good night, each of them soon falling into trouble-free slumber.

However, her burden did not ease.

≈

Derek watched the back of the wagon where Penny had disappeared, no longer interested in his map. It told him nothing he needed from the day's travel, and again he speculated on whether he'd been fooled into some wild goose chase for a nonexistent fortune in silver.

He recalled Penny's words, muted but understandable, as she'd read to her girls just like his ma had done with him when he was a boy. He'd recognized the stories and felt a sweet nostalgia upon hearing them again, remembering how his ma chided him when she'd caught him in some mischief and often compared his misdeeds to one of the parables Jesus taught. At one point, Derek had begun to think of himself as the prodigal son, though he wasn't the one who'd left home—his pa had done that. But as often as his ma recounted that story, he'd figured she was trying to get some sort of message across.

A stir at the canvas brought his attention from the fire where it had wandered back to the wagon. Hurriedly, he folded the map sections and tucked them inside his buckskin jacket under one of his suspenders as the Widow Crawder climbed down from the wagon bed. She looked his way, as if uncertain, before approaching him.

"I want to express my thanks once more for what you did for Olivia," she explained.

"Well, ma'am." He rose to stand, a bit embarrassed by all the fuss she made out of the incident. "Isn't that what you hired me for? As an extra gun for protection?"

"Aye. Be that as it may, when I asked you to join us and thought of the girls needing protection, I had in mind the two-legged variety of predator, not the. . .however many-legged thing that vile creature was. I never stopped to consider that the dangers are unending no matter how careful we are." She looked off to the side in the direction of a black mass of hills that blocked out part of the nighttime sky as if trying to search out the answers to her problems there.

After a moment, she cleared her throat, returning her attention to him. "Also, I want to say. . .that is, I wish to tell you. . ." She took a deep breath and rolled her glance up to the stars, clearly ill at ease. "I wish to apologize for prying into your affairs yet again. Three times I've done so, and I haven't the right. 'Tis a fact, one shouldn't judge a man by his past, as my da used to say. . .whatever your past may be.

So it is irrelevant. You've proven to me twice over that you're a man who can be trusted."

He studied her, mystified as to what she had in mind now. "I appreciate the apology, but there's no need. I wouldn't have told you anything if I hadn't wanted to."

She blinked. "Oh. All right then. Well, I'll be wishing you a pleasant evening, Mr. Burke." She nodded a hasty farewell and turned to go, then turned around, her motion as swift. "One last matter, then I'll be leavin' you to your. . .whatever you may have been doing. Not that I'm asking." She paused to allow a response, but when he offered none, she cleared her throat and continued. "Aye, well I plan to read to the girls from the Bible of a morning before we break the fast, and I'd like to issue an invitation for you to join us. Only if you'd care to attend; I'm not forcing the matter."

"Thank you, ma'am. I'll consider it."

Derek watched her retrace her steps to her wagon and wondered if she considered him a soul in need of reforming and if that had been the driving force behind her sudden invitation. He feared God but didn't trust Him, nor did he believe God cared anything about him. And he doubted if the Widow Crawder could change his mind in that regard. Even so, he supposed it would be impolite to decline her charitable, if awkward, offer. Besides, likely nothing existed in the Good Book that he hadn't heard his mother tell him before.

seven

The miles of tedium progressed, and their sightings of game diminished. With no meat, Penny made do with johnnycakes cooked in her three-legged, cast-iron spider. What stores remained of flour, coffee, and other staples had been acquired during Oliver's trip into Silverton last year, and she hoped to replenish her supplies once she arrived in Carson City—or perhaps at a trading post if they came across a town. At least the blisters on her fingers from holding the reins had toughened, and she felt thankful for small blessings.

Each morning, Penny read a chapter aloud from the Bible. She'd decided against doing so before breakfast, with the hope that everyone could then concentrate on the readings and not the rumblings in their stomachs. Nevertheless, Derek still seemed jittery when she read, and she wondered if he didn't often get a chance to hear the Good Book's wisdom. Or perhaps he felt uncomfortable standing for so long in respect for the occasion. No matter, Penny couldn't place blame. She should have furthered her girls' spiritual instruction instead of distancing herself from God. On this journey through nowhere, she felt as if she was once more beginning to find Him.

On the seventh morning, they reached a bluff and had to leave the river behind to take a cutoff. For what seemed like endless miles, they traveled up and down some of the steepest and most stony terrain Penny had ever encountered. At times, she wasn't sure the horses could manage the hills, and Derek needed to lead her team on foot, his horse tied to the wagon.

Through her da's tales, she'd learned of the cutoff and also that an additional day's journey would bring them to a canyon with a treasure. Not silver or even gold. But instead, hidden at the edge of a hill, a sheltered pool of heated water bubbled up from beneath the earth, protected from the sun's rays.

At this point, any water would be welcome water, even hot.

Finally, they came to a spring that, although fresh, turned out to be muddy. Seeing no feed for the horses, they rested only long enough for Penny to collect and boil water for their containers and for the horses to take their fill from the watering place. They traveled another few miles and returned to the river where, exhausted, they stayed the night.

❧

Long before the rising sun glazed the rocks with vibrant rose, Penny awoke, weary but determined, and set to work making breakfast. Grateful to note the cloud banks to the west, thicker than the wispy trails of the past week, she hoped they would act as a shield against the sun since she doubted they would produce rain. The land seldom received it.

While the wagon rolled forward along the plain, her mind revisited former years. She replayed memorable events: the happy ones when she'd married Oliver and given birth to each of her children, and the most tragic moments when she'd buried her stillborn son and two years later her husband, after bites from a rattlesnake had killed him. Even if she'd reached Oliver in time, she doubted she could have saved him with her plant cures.

Her father's lilting words came back to her in the midst of her sorrowful daydream: *"Ye need t' get a grip on the reins o' your life, lassie, no matter which way the trail takes you. Yer the only one who can."*

That was what she was trying to do, wasn't she? Guide their destiny rather than sit on the outskirts and let the future be wrested from her hands? At times, she could convince herself of that, but at night as she tried to sleep while the distant, wavering howls of coyotes sounded far beyond their camp, her heart accused her of giving up and letting *them* win. And when that happened, the old fears and bitterness she kept buried deep inside festered like a poison, the pain so intense she thought her heart might stop.

What made her think life would be any different in Carson City? Had she been rash to sweep her girls away from what had been home for more than ten years?

"No matter; what's done is done," she assured herself under her breath, using her da's words. Some semblance of law must abide in such a large city, contrary to what Derek led her to believe. Surely a widow with two small children wouldn't be preyed upon, robbed, or harmed in an attempt to run them out of house and home. Her recent troubles of the hatred and bias they'd endured from a select few heathens settled like a thick, noxious brew in her throat, as if to strangle her.

"Mama, did you say something?" Christa asked from the wagon seat beside her.

"Hand me the water container, please."

Her daughter took the buffalo skin from her lap and offered it to her ma.

Taking in slow, deep breaths to try to ease the lump in her throat, then a sip of water when that didn't reduce it, Penny resolved to forget the pile of ruins that cluttered the life she'd left. Instead, she would concentrate on the flicker of hope that beckoned her forward to a future in Carson City. It was the only right thing to do: leave her troubles behind. Why, then, didn't that knowledge alleviate her every qualm?

Morning passed into afternoon, and afternoon into early evening, until finally they reached the canyon as the sun began its gradual drop to the western horizon.

"Christa, do you see how the rocks and sagebrush form at the top of those hills to look like horns and eyes? It brings to mind a buffalo head." Another landmark about which her da had told her.

"Do you think I'll see a buffalo some day? Maybe in Carson City?"

Penny glanced at her youngest. "Maybe." The buffalo had long disappeared from this part of the land, killed off in droves; Penny hadn't seen one since she was Christa's age.

Engrossed in thought, she almost missed the huge gray boulders of cliff that rose from the ground, one almost rectangular like a door, the other two cut out of the hill to angle on either side and atop it. "Three Leaning Rocks" her da had called it. A thread of sentimentality to know her father once camped here wove around Penny, making her feel close to him.

She looked at her daughter, noting her flushed cheeks. "Are you feeling any better?"

Christa nodded. "My stomach doesn't hurt no more."

"Anymore." Penny smiled. "Please tell Mr. Burke I'd like to stop here for the night." She hoped Derek would agree. From the sun's position in the sky, they still had an hour or so before they usually made camp.

Christa slipped off the slow-moving wagon to the ground and scampered to where Derek rode about fifteen feet ahead.

He also looked to the right, to the outcropping of rocks. As Olivia delivered Penny's message, he turned to her girl for the brief moment it took to answer, then looked back at the three rocks.

Penny wondered what about them he found so fascinating. They were rocks like any other; only she guessed what lay beyond that hill.

Christa scampered back to the wagon. "He said that would be fine."

"Good. Now go check if Olivia's caught anything." Christa ran to the back of the wagon, and Penny drew her team to a halt. She kept quiet as they made camp and noticed Derek's frequent glances of puzzlement turned her way mixed with what appeared to be a measure of concern. Her frequent ponderings had triggered a personal melancholy she couldn't seem to shake.

"Mama." Olivia cradled her arm, walking up to Penny as she unpacked utensils from the box. "I'm sorry I didn't catch the rabbit I saw. And now I can't catch anything. It hurts to hold my slingshot."

"What did you do to yourself, Livvie?" Penny held her daughter's arm up for observation, noting the reddish bruise on her forearm and wrist.

"I was running after a rabbit, and I fell." Olivia's face was downcast as if she'd committed some grievous blunder.

"That's all right, love." She pressed her palm against Olivia's cheek. " 'Tis a wee bit swollen, but only bruised, not broken. I'll make a salve for the pain. And it certainly won't hurt us to have another evening without meat."

Olivia didn't look convinced. "Maybe Mr. Burke will go and hunt us up something?" she suggested hopefully. Penny knew her daughter wasn't fond of the johnnycakes prepared with flour and water. They didn't hold together well and tasted bland, even with salt.

"I'm sure he would if we ask, but we shouldn't trouble him. He's done enough."

"What shouldn't you trouble me about?" Derek came up behind them, almost startling Penny out of her skin. She looked at him, and he gave an awkward smile. "I imagine you were talking about me, being as I'm the only male for miles around."

"Actually we were, but—"

"I was hoping you might go hunting so we don't have to eat johnnycakes again," Olivia interrupted with her usual forthrightness, earning a stern glance from Penny. "I saw a rabbit, so I know there's animals around here somewhere, but I hurt myself—see?" She held her arm up for his observation. "But Ma said I shouldn't ask 'cause you helped us so much already."

"Well now," he started, and Penny couldn't mistake the amusement glimmering in his eyes. "Your ma's johnnycakes aren't so bad, not like some of the doughy lumps I've had in my lifetime. But I don't mind going out to look for dinner."

"Or perhaps I should look for an anthill and gather up the ants there to brown in a skillet for a change of course to please my finicky daughter?" Penny said in quiet reprimand. "That's what my grandmother and her tribe ate when food was scarce."

"Eww," Christa intoned, joining them as Penny spoke. Her youngest wrinkled her nose in distaste.

Olivia dropped her gaze, shamefaced. "I'm sorry, Mama. I try to be thankful for the food the good Lord's given us.

Honest, I do. I'm not trying to be ill-mannered or greedy. But is it so awful to wish for something that tastes good and don't have dirt in it?"

Olivia did have a point. Dust granules found their way into everything, even the food supplies.

"I don't mind," Derek inserted. "As a matter of fact, I'd like to scout around, see what's behind them hills. Animals use the rocks for shade. Snakes, too."

"Eww." Christa again made her idea plain on the subject of dinner.

He grinned. "Aw, rattlesnake meat isn't so bad. Tastes like tough chicken."

Penny inwardly shuddered. She'd eaten snake before, but with the recent memory of her husband's demise, the thought of rattlesnake for a meal didn't sit well. "I'm not sure it's wise to leave the trail and go scouting through the canyon. Other forms of life use the hills for places to hide, too." She thought of the warring renegades but kept her words vague so as not to frighten her girls. "Christa, go with Olivia and bring me my box of plant cuttings. I'll make that salve for you."

The girls hurried off, and she made quick use of her words, taking little care how she delivered them. "How do you know you might not come face to face with a renegade in war paint or, God forbid, a war party? I dinnae think you should hunt in such concealed areas where you could wind up cornered and scalped. If you went and got yourself killed, what good would that do any of us, I ask you?"

He regarded her with amused disbelief; that same hint of merriment lit his eyes and flickered at the corners of his mouth. "Ma'am, I assure you I can take care of myself. Been doing it for years and plan to for many more. Maybe you hadn't heard, cut off like you were, but since the Paiute War ended a number of years ago, there hasn't been much trouble reported in this part of the West. Many of the natives hereabouts have gone to live on reservations."

"Believe me, Mr. Burke, if anyone knows that, I do." She hadn't heard news in well over a year regarding the conflict between the natives and the settlers, but his words brought slim reassurance. Peace treaties with many tribes had formed at other times in the past, and some misunderstanding had erupted, leading to yet another war. Pocatello, a chief of the Northwestern Shoshone where her grandmother Kimama had come from, once engaged in massacres against the emigrants before taking his people to Fort Hall Reservation for fear of starvation. "It is not the supporters of peace of whom I speak."

"Who then? Red Cloud? I doubt the warrior chief of the Sioux abandoned his lands to ride south to Nevada and hide behind this particular group of hills."

She bristled, recognizing enjoyment in his voice. He seemed in quite the cheerful mood—more so than she'd ever seen him. His eyes fairly radiated with energy, odd after such a long day's travel.

"Mr. Burke, are you ridiculing me for my ignorance of the situation?"

His smile faded. "No, ma'am. Sorry you took it that way." He looked toward the nearest hill, rife with boulders, his expression pensive. "As a matter of fact, I found myself in a skirmish with Red Cloud and his band of warriors a few years back when I rode with a group of men who took the Bozeman Trail."

"What happened?" Penny was almost afraid to ask.

"I was one of the lucky ones. Most were killed in the attack;

the U.S. Cavalry arrived just in time to save me my scalp. Last I heard, Red Cloud is still waging war in his demand that the military remove their forts from the Powder River territory."

"Aye," she said distantly. "'Tis a difficult state of affairs to be sure. My husband believed that both sides have been in error throughout this entire conflict of wars, ever since the settlers first came to the West."

"I reckon that's so."

"You do?" Penny hadn't expected that. The rare times she'd ridden into Silverton with Oliver, some of the miners' hateful looks made it clear exactly which nation they blamed. And her grandmother's people had been one of the peaceful tribes, negating war.

"I've heard talk in my travels. Neither side has been without its share of blame," he said. This time she couldn't mask her surprise, and he lifted his brows in question. "You think just because my skin is white I can't reason out the facts that my own eyes and ears tell me?"

"No, it's not that. It's just. . .my husband thought the same way, as did my father. Not many people do."

"You never talk much about your husband." His words came soft, a prod she chose to acknowledge.

"Oliver was a quiet man who believed in the Bible, in the Almighty God, and in all He said about men being equal through Christ." She smiled, remembering his gentle nature but fervent heart. "He met my da at the trading post, and I was with him at the time. They bonded at once, finding like-minded kinship and speaking of what was then and still is the talk in these parts—the ongoing wars with the natives and expansion of the West. Oliver came by wagon train with his family and planned to travel farther, but he ended up finding a home here. It may seem odd, to claim a dwelling in such a barren land, but my father had ties here, and I formed them, too. Oliver respected that."

"Your grandmother's people." His words were a statement, almost gentle.

"Aye, though I've seldom seen them since my da died. They have gone to a reservation north of here."

"And Oliver?"

"He came to respect the land, though it never yielded much harvest to him."

"But you stayed."

"Aye." She looked toward the hill of rocks. "This land can be brutal, even dangerous, but it contains a fierce beauty I respect. When the sagebrush blooms along the hills and wildflowers of all colors flood the valleys, it near takes my breath away. This land can even seem gentle, such as when the tamarisk blooms a soft rose in cloudy plumes like fans of feathers. I wouldn't wish to live elsewhere." Conscious of her faraway, rambling manner, she made mockery of her words. "Och, don't be mindin' me blather. Waxing poetic, that's the Scots in me. With the native ways I learned from my mother and my grandfather, even my da, we survived. And I will go on surviving," she added as an afterthought.

"I don't doubt it. You have the tenacity of a mule."

The words hardly flattered, but she couldn't mistake the admiration in his eyes and voice. His lips twitched as he sought to restrain a smile. "You're like this land of yours. Fierce, strong, dangerous but admirable. . ." His words trailed off as if he would add more. With the manner in which his eyes gentled, intent on her face, she thought he might say *beautiful*. But he didn't.

Before she could manage a reply that wouldn't cue him in to her strange and sudden discomfiture, the girls returned from the back of the wagon with the box of cuttings, and Derek stepped away. "I'll be going now."

"Don't feel you must," Penny hurried to say.

"I wouldn't mind a nice rabbit roasted in your spices myself." He gave a parting nod and strode away.

"You ought not to have said anything, Olivia," Penny chastised once he was out of hearing range.

"Please don't be mad, Mama. I didn't mean any harm." Olivia held her injured wrist, her soft brown eyes pleading for forgiveness. "But won't it be nice to have meat again? I think it'll help Christa, too. She's been acting all tuckered out lately."

Penny glanced at Christa, concerned, as she had been ever since Christa had chosen to ride rather than walk. Perhaps Olivia was right.

She tried hard to act grown-up but was still so much the little girl, and Penny didn't have the heart to scold her elder daughter further. Olivia and Christa had been through so much, more than any children should have to suffer. Losing their pa and the following year reaping the hatred of men without fully understanding why had left a brand of injury on their own hearts.

She gave Olivia a slight smile. "I suppose it will help Christa to feel better. Aye."

Penny lifted the hinged lid of her box and noted the dirt caked into her hands and forearms. She wished to clean off the ever-present dust and grime that had blown against her and buried deep inside the crevices of her skin, sullying her skirts and smudging the gray cloth with brown. Morning, noon, and night, she could taste the dust in her mouth, her teeth gritty from the exposure. Derek assured her no dangers from warring tribes or renegades existed in this area, and likely he'd heard more recent news and been better informed than she, since he was a drifter who traveled from town to town. Given that he showed no qualms to go off exploring, she decided her anxiety must reside only within her mind and determined such fears would end here and now.

Penny mashed roots of the yellow dock she'd gathered days ago and applied the paste to Olivia's swollen wrist. As she bound a strip of cloth around it, Penny issued strict orders for Olivia and Christa to remain inside the wagon, even giving permission for Olivia to retrieve whichever of two books from the trunk she chose to read to her little sister—a McGuffey's reader that had belonged to her husband, or a book of poetry her da had given her mother. Her da traded with a wagonload of pioneers for it and other books, as well as for a few bolts of pretty sprigged material and a fancy silver hand mirror with engraved swirls and flowers etched into the heavy metal. All the possessions had become a burden to the California-bound travelers who'd needed to shed weight in order to complete their journey, but they proved a delight to Penny's mother. Penny could still remember her exclamations of joy with each parcel opened—as if Christmas had come early—and how once her da saw Penny in her new blue calico dress, he'd lifted her high in his brawny arms, near to the ceiling. With her giggling the entire time, he'd swung her around the room, singing to her that she was the "finest wee bonnie lass in all the Nevada Territory."

"Mama?" Judging from Olivia's wide-eyed expression, she was astounded by the unexpected privilege of reading the treasured books. At least her tears had dried, brave though she'd been in not uttering a sound the entire time Penny had treated her injured wrist.

"Aye, you heard correctly." Penny knotted the ends of the cloth. "Go off with you then."

"Thank you, Mama!" With a smile, Olivia scampered away.

Unable to shake the longing, Penny glanced toward the tall canyon wall of shielding rock and sagebrush, in the opposite direction Derek had taken. Surely it would take time to hunt game, since sightings had been so scarce. What she wouldn't give for that feeling of contentment, to be safe and loved again, and for a cleansing bath as well. Perhaps she could not have the one. . .but she could very well do something about the other.

eight

Derek found their dinner a lot faster than he would have imagined after not having seen hide nor hair of one wild critter all day. The rabbit raced across his path when he'd ridden a bare mile from camp, and he wondered if it was the same one Olivia had spotted. Now he hoped for an early dinner and could imagine the meat rubbed with Penny's herbs and baked over a slow fire. His mouth watered just thinking about it. He peered at the stands of rocky, scrub-covered hills that stood at least two-stories tall on either side.

Unless he missed his guess, those three odd rocks in the hill nearest the wagon were exactly like the shape of the ones on his pa's map, near what looked like a sketch of the cutoff they'd taken; and if that was the case, he was headed in the right direction. The X marked on the map went westward from the pile of rocks nearly the length of his little finger, then hooked up to the north. Whether that distance meant a few miles or days, he had no way of telling, and he also wondered why he, Clay, and Linda had been instructed to meet in Silverton rather than at a more local mining camp or town, since Nevada teemed with them from what he'd seen in his travels. Surely, as far as they'd gone, there must be one nearby. But then, there was no way of telling what scheme his pa had cooked up at the time he'd sketched the map, or why.

From this angle, Derek noticed Olivia and Christa, their skirts and moccasin-clad feet dangling out the back of the wagon where they sat, but he saw no sign of their mother. As he rode closer, Olivia looked up and spotted him. A smile spread across her face when she shifted her gaze to the rabbit slung across his saddle. She jumped down from the wagon and closed the distance, Christa following her lead and running at a slower pace.

"Will this do?" Derek lifted the rabbit by its back paws when both girls stopped near his horse.

Christa let out a squeal of delight and jumped up and down, clapping her hands. Derek was relieved to see a more rose color to her face than the unhealthy pallor it had taken on at the noon break. He guessed the sagebrush leaves her ma'd had her chew helped to correct whatever had ailed her.

"I reckon it will, then," he chuckled, holding his find out to them.

Olivia took the carcass with her unbandaged hand, her eyes gleaming with appreciation. "Aye," she said, sounding like her ma. "That'll do right well, Mr. Burke! No more of them awful johnnycakes tonight."

Derek looked past her, expecting to see Penny walk from around the wagon. When she didn't appear, he drew his brows downward in a puzzled frown and, calling out her name, guided his horse to the other side of the wagon. The area was empty except for more sagebrush and rocks.

"Where's your ma?"

"She took her shotgun and went behind that hill." Olivia nodded in the opposite direction from where Derek had gone.

"She told us we weren't to move a hair from the wagon," Christa added shyly, smiling at Derek. "And that she'd be back soon."

"Behind that hill there?" Bewilderment made Derek lean

forward in his saddle. "Why would she do that?" He wondered if she had decided to try her hand at hunting game, but that didn't sound like Penny.

"Don't know," Olivia said with a shrug.

"Don't know," Christa mimicked her big sister.

Derek frowned, his attention wheeling back to the hill with the three odd rocks. What business could Penny have wandering off like she did? He couldn't see any plants from this point, nothing different from what grew nearby, so she sure couldn't have seen anything to add to her box of cuttings.

He dismounted and tied his horse to the back of the wagon. "You girls stay out of trouble while I skin this rabbit. Olivia, you might lend a hand by doing whatever it is your ma has you do to get a meal ready."

"I can help! I can make the meal, too. Mama showed me how." With an eager light in her eyes, Olivia scrambled to the back of the wagon and began to pull out utensils with one hand.

"Me, too!" Christa called and ran after her sister, dropping her doll and stopping to pick it up again before joining Olivia.

Derek wondered if Olivia was as gifted a cook as her ma; it would be a shame to let such a coveted find burn to a cinder. He glanced toward the hill again before he withdrew his knife and made quick work of preparing the rabbit for cooking. Afterward, he collected greasewood to start a fire. When Penny still hadn't returned once the flames flickered low beneath the gathered brush, worry began to gnaw at his gut.

"How long ago did your ma leave?"

"Not long before you got back." Olivia's attention remained on the meat she placed inside the black pot. She wrinkled her brow, as if indecisive, then grabbed the long fork and stuck it into the meat.

He studied the rocks again. "I'm going to look for her. You girls stay by the wagon, like she said. Don't wander off."

"Oh, I won't. I have plenty to keep me busy." With her uninjured hand, Olivia proudly held up the long fork with which she'd impaled the skinned rabbit. The carcass fell off the two tines and at her feet. "Oops. Guess I didn't poke it through hard enough." She picked it up, brushing off the dirt that had caked onto the flesh.

This didn't bode well.

"I'll hurry."

Derek took off in the direction Olivia had shown him and stepped through the narrow gap between hills, with room for only one person to walk. He had to climb over rocks before again meeting level ground. Why on God's green earth would the woman take it into her head to go off exploring, especially when she'd been opposed to the idea? He stepped sideways along the rough ground, squeezing past a narrow crevice. Beyond that, more rocks stood close together. From somewhere distant, he heard something out of place. Coming to a halt, he waited, silent, straining to hear. A woman's faint groan reached him.

Realizing Penny was in trouble, Derek quickened his pace, his hand going to the handle of his gun.

⋅❧⋅

Penny awoke from partial slumber, letting out a sigh of sheer contentment as she delighted in the silky water of the small, shallow pool. Hot, but not uncomfortably so, the springs bore the smell of rust and eggs, but she didn't mind. She'd found the hidden oasis with little trouble and submersed herself wearing only her chemise, figuring it the best washing it would receive at this point. She should get back, she reasoned.

On the heels of that thought, she again heard the lilting trill of the girls' faraway laughter echo off the canyon walls, assuring her all was well at camp.

Perhaps just one minute more. . .

Again she swept up the thick fall of her hair and held it atop her head with one hand, rescuing the bottom tendrils that had fallen and gotten wet when she'd nodded off. Letting her neck rest against the smooth rock, she smiled and issued another sigh of pleasure, closing her eyes.

"Ah, Da, you were right. This is pure bliss."

Her grandmother's people used hot springs like this one for cleansing of body and spirit, and she could certainly use a dousing for both. She recalled a verse Oliver often quoted from Psalms and whispered it now, "Create in me a clean heart, O God; and renew a right spirit within me." Up until that moment, she hadn't realized how much she needed renewal and how like this land—parched and arid—her spirit had become.

Her da had mentioned the location of the springs through accounts of his travels. He'd found it purely by accident, and she wondered if anyone else knew of its existence. Before this, Penny had never visited a spring and wished now that she might live near one in the future. Every taut muscle in her body relaxed, soothed by the hot water that made her feel as light as the very air. Had the day been as miserable as the previous, she wouldn't have been able to bear it, but she'd been fortunate that the thick clouds had stolen some of the heat from the afternoon.

The crunch of hurried footsteps brought her upright in the water with a jump. Her neck and bare shoulders broke the surface, the dripping sleeves of her chemise pulled down by the weight of the water. Sure that her adventuresome girls had disobeyed and followed, she primed herself to deliver a scolding, when suddenly her intruder appeared from beyond the shielding rock, a gun aimed in her direction.

Her brown eyes met the startled blue ones of their guide.

They stared at one another for a few shocked seconds before Derek spun around at the same time Penny immersed her body completely beneath the surface until her mouth skimmed water. The action to dunk came without thought, and she strangled on the water she'd inhaled. As she groped to sit up, her hair fell in.

"Sorry, ma'am," he mumbled, replacing his gun in his holster. Clearly awkward and undecided, he raised his hand and swept it along his nape, knocking his hat awry, then settled both hands at his hips.

"What are you doing here?" she managed once she could stop coughing.

"I heard you moan. I. . .uh. . .thought you were in danger or hurt," he stammered without turning around. "I figure you're not, though."

"No, I'm fine." Embarrassed that he'd heard her enjoyment of what she'd thought to be a private moment, she slid down against the smooth rock until her chin skimmed water. Something he said didn't ring quite true. "You heard me from the campsite and came to investigate?" She didn't think her expressions of delight could have carried that far, but then again, she'd heard the girls' laughter from here.

"Not exactly. I was looking for you."

"Looking for me?" Dread pricked her conscience. "The girls, they're okay?" She never should have left them alone, not after the scorpion scare almost a week before. What had she been thinking? Yet neither did she want to smother them or allow her maternal fears to resurface and control her. She hadn't thought they could get into trouble reading a book inside the wagon, though.

"The girls are fine. They didn't seem to know much about where you'd gone or why, and it made me wonder." Hands still straddling his hips, he looked up at the sky, craning his neck as if to get rid of a crick. "Look, this was a big blunder on my part. I. . .uh. . .should go now. Yeah, I should go." Before she could respond, he hurriedly moved out of sight. "You might want to return soon," he called from behind the hill. "Olivia has it in mind that she's going to cook dinner."

"I've taught her some, so she should be able to take over," she called back, then remembered her daughter's injured wrist. "Aye, I'll be there soon."

Penny remained as motionless as the rocks around her, wanting to make sure he was well and truly gone. Her mind replayed the incident until she could begin to see the humor, enough so that she smiled. The poor man seemed far more embarrassed than she. It could have been worse; Derek could have caught her in a mortifying state of complete undress rather than covered in her chemise and immersed in water up to her shoulders. Such musings made her feel a bit more poised and able to face him again.

Penny wondered if he'd found game; he hadn't mentioned it, and in the embarrassment of the moment, she hadn't thought to ask. She certainly hadn't thought he would return so soon from his hunt or she would have never allowed herself the luxury of a bath.

She stepped out of the pool, her eyes keeping wary watch on the shielding slab of sandstone around which he'd disappeared. She didn't really think he would come back;

he seemed too honorable to do something of that sort. She ducked behind another large slab of rock, nonetheless, to pull off the dripping chemise that no longer ballooned around her but stuck to her like a second skin. With no toweling with which to dry off, she made do with the cleaner inside of her skirt, then snatched her mother's dress from atop a boulder nearby and struggled into it. The supple doeskin hugged her form, and she appreciated its velvet-soft texture. She smoothed the material over her hips, then sat down to pull on and lace her moccasins.

In the dress, Penny wondered if she favored her mother. The desire to feel more like a woman coupled with her girls' eager suggestion she wear it helped to ease her mind as to whether she was being foolish. They'd both smiled when she took it from the trunk earlier, along with the two books she'd promised them. Now, as she combed her fingers through her wet hair, working out the tangles from her crown to below her waist, she wished she had a looking glass or some other method to see her reflection. Her mother's silver mirror had cracked years before when Olivia, a little whirlwind even at age three, accidentally dropped it.

Not keen to waste further time with braiding her hair or pinning it up, Penny bundled the dirty clothes and wet chemise under her arm, grabbed her shotgun, and headed back, deciding she would return and wash her clothes before they left in the morning. And the girls should have a good bath, too.

As Penny approached camp, Derek looked up from where he cooked something over a fire. The surprised appreciation in his eyes encouraged her that she'd made a worthwhile choice.

Olivia's mouth dropped open. "Mama, you look so pretty."

"Pretty Mama!" Christa's smile was wide.

Derek continued to stare.

Flustered by all the attention, Penny looked to the fire. "I see you found dinner, but you shouldn't be doing that. That's what I'm here for." She tried to take the fork with the hunk of whatever meat he'd found away from him, but he shook his head.

"I don't mind. I figured you could use the rest." Their eyes met; behind his intent gaze, she could tell he also recalled their recent encounter and her "rest" there. Her face grew hotter, and his went a tinge darker as he glanced away, back to the meat baking over the flames. "So you might as well claim a patch of dirt, sit, and rest your heels for a spell while I'm in this frame of mind," he added.

Silence settled between them, thick and uneasy, while Penny's thoughts thrummed like a ceremonial drum inside her head. Relaxation was the last thing she needed with her mind all aflutter. She preferred to keep her hands just as busy and strode to the wagon to collect the eating utensils. Out of sight of the others, she pressed her fingers to her warm cheeks, chiding herself for her wayward recollections, which seemed intent on taking her back to the awkward moment they shared.

They needed a diversion. But what, in the middle of this wilderness, could be used for diversionary purposes? She looked at the trunk a moment, then opened it. Her eyes fell upon her da's mouth organ. He hadn't been the best of musicians by his own confession, but music, even poorly played, had always served to fill lengthy gaps of quiet.

Ignoring the box of plates, Penny reached for the harmonica partially twined within a necklace of miniature blue and red glass beads that once belonged to her mother. She pulled them out as well and stared at them. Perhaps because they went with the dress or perhaps because she felt caught up in memories of the past, she slid them over her head and pulled her thick hair from beneath the strand. She then polished the silver instrument, rubbing it against the soft leather of her skirt, as fond memories of her da caused her lips to turn up in a bittersweet smile. Olivia had been learning to play years ago but had lost interest shortly after Penny's father died. Perhaps she could talk her daughter into treating them to a tune or two.

She returned to Derek and the girls, who both talked around the fire.

"What have you got there, Mama?" Christa asked, her gaze dropping to Penny's hand.

"This belonged to your grandda," Penny said with a smile.

"I haven't seen one of those in years," Derek mused. "Not since the one I had."

"You play?" Penny asked in some surprise.

"It's been a while." His eyes remained on the harmonica. "I was a boy, not that much older than Olivia. I haven't touched one since then."

"My da didn't play much in the years before his heart gave out; just a tune now and then. He wasn't that accomplished, either, though I did love to hear him play when I was a child."

"Who said I wasn't accomplished?" Derek's smirk boded mischief.

"You said you only played when you were a boy."

"Responsibility comes with a hard price; I didn't have time to play after my pa left." After his curious explanation, he turned to Olivia. "Think you can handle a turn at holding this?"

"Oh, sure. My wrist feels a wee bit better." She moved closer to Derek, taking the long fork with the browning meat on it.

He held out his hand to Penny. "Mind if I give it a try?"

She offered him the instrument. He took it, turned it over in his hands a few times, then put it to his lips and blew. The resulting discordant notes brought a giggle from Christa.

"All right there, little moppet," he teased. "Just give me a minute. I didn't say I wasn't rusty."

Penny's heart tugged at the pet name he called her daughter, and she wondered if he'd begun to regard them from a viewpoint other than that of a guide. The more she got to know him, the more she approved of what she saw. The girls were fond of him; he seemed to get along and connect with them in some manner that she hadn't seen since their pa died. Still, she and the girls had lived cut off from everyone and shared little contact with any man other than the pitiless miners whose sole connection had been mutual hatred. It wasn't so difficult to understand why her girls would be drawn to Derek's kindness. But the fact remained: The girls needed a pa, and Penny needed a husband. She further dwelled on the idea of Derek filling that gap in their lives.

After a few more awkward wails, a sudden string of lyrical notes trembled through the air, resounding off the canyon walls, and he went into a rollicking tune that had Christa jump up from the ground and spin around in a loose form of a Scottish reel. "Dance with me, Mama!" she laughed, grabbing Penny's arm. "Show me how again!"

Infused with Christa's contagious enthusiasm and delighted to see her feeling well, Penny laughed and linked elbows with her daughter, twirling her round and then in the direction opposite in a dance her da had taught her from his homeland.

Olivia, too, became caught up in the excitement, her feet moving in rhythm, so much so that she dropped the meat in the fire.

"Oh, my!" she cried.

Derek ceased entertaining them and saved their supper from becoming charred ruins.

"I'm sorry," Olivia rushed to say, her face twisted as though she might cry. "I didn't mean to drop it."

"Nothing to worry your head over," Derek responded with a smile her way. "I like my meat well done."

Olivia grinned. "Will you play some more?"

Penny gave a slight, disbelieving shake of her head, again amazed at how well Derek related to her girls for being such a self-declared loner. But in the best interest of their meal, she suggested they save further music until after dinner.

The rest of the evening unfolded in a relaxed atmosphere missing on previous days, and Penny could almost imagine them as a family. Derek teased the girls and told them stories of his travels, much like her da had done when she was a child. Once their stomachs were filled, with everyone content, she washed the dishes with sand and water, tapping her foot in rhythm while Derek played the harmonica and her girls danced with one another to the lilting melodies. Every time Penny glanced his way, she noticed him watching her, though she couldn't place the look in his eyes. Curiosity? Interest? Confusion?

She wished she could read him, but he remained a mystery.

A mystery much like the length of folded paper she'd glimpsed him pull from his saddlebag late the previous evening as she'd studied him from inside the back of her wagon. He'd sat near the fire and stared at it a long time without opening it, his features somber, before stuffing the paper back into the casing, unread. Somehow she didn't think he carried a packet of poems. She hoped he wasn't pining over a love letter, though he'd told her no special woman had appealed enough to make him want to change his course.

But what if his course contained a case of unrequited love? He had seemed rather curt with his answers on the evening she'd sought them.

Penny transferred her feelings to the kettle as she scrubbed it out hard and hoped that a woman from his past had not already laid claim to Derek's heart.

nine

Once twilight settled its blanket of dusky purple over the land, and Olivia and Christa said their good nights and headed for the wagon, Penny sat down near the fire to rest.

"It's so pretty out tonight, so peaceful," she mused, staring up at the scattering of stars that glittered above the hills. She turned her head to look at Derek, who sat on the ground nearby. "I must admit, Mr. Burke, you're good with my girls. I'm surprised; you don't seem the type to be a loner. . .sorry." She recalled her promise not to interfere. "Forget I spoke."

He continued staring into the fire, his lips pursed in that amused, resigned manner with which she was fast becoming familiar. Her apology seemed destined to fade into darkness along with the smoke before he gave a brief, decisive nod and looked at her. His lips quirked again and squeezed into a smile. What was it about that small mannerism of his that made her heart give a couple of quick thuds? Preposterous! She, a widow and the mother of two small children, was not a besotted young girl.

"I was born in a small lean-to in the Ozarks, the eldest son of an Irish immigrant and an English schoolteacher," Derek said in a slow drawl. "One day, Pa heard news of the Comstock Lode and got it into his head he no longer needed a family. He headed west to mine for silver. I was fourteen at the time."

"Excuse me?" Penny asked in bewilderment, her mind

stalling at his swift change of topic.

"You wanted to know my past."

"Aye, but it isn't any of my business, as I said before." Flustered by his blunt comment, she focused on smoothing the wrinkles from her dress. "Please don't feel obliged to tell me."

"You no longer interested?"

"Well, no, I didn't say that."

He barely lifted his brow, giving her an intent look as if his mind worked hard to get her preferences straight. "Which I take to mean that you'd like to know more?"

She hesitated, loath to utter the smallest fib. "Well now, if you're of a mind to tell me your story, Mr. Burke, I wouldna be ignoring you."

He grinned at that. "You're a peculiar woman, Penny Crawder."

They both seemed a bit startled by his slip of familiarity in using her Christian name. Before he could apologize, she raised her hand to stop him.

"Out in this wilderness and taking into account all we've been through together, it seems strange to stand on formalities. You may call me Penny." She smiled at his assenting nod. "And before I'll be forgetting, I would be most interested to hear what you mean by calling me 'peculiar'."

He let out a laugh, rich and deep but low enough to not wake the girls. The masculine sound of it lit something sweet and warm within her belly, making her smile.

"Oh, I doubt there'd be any likelihood of you forgetting anything when you latch your mind onto it. And I mean that in the nicest way possible." The glint in his eye was roguish, and she did what came naturally. She leaned over and swatted his arm in mock annoyance as though they'd known each other for years. A bit stunned by her spontaneous act, she waited to see how he would respond, but he only dipped his head with another flicker of his lips, as if trying to mask his amusement.

"Well, bein' as how you've introduced the subject a second time, and not I, would you be holdin' any resentment toward me if I were to ask a wee bit more concerning your family?"

His smile grew as he looked at her.

"What?" she asked, wondering what she'd said that made him smile so.

"Did you know when you get anxious or excited, the Scot in you comes out?"

"Does it now? Well, I suppose I have my da to thank for that, bein' as he was the one to raise me."

"I like it," he stunned her by saying. "That, mixed with your Indian heritage, is all a part of what makes you special. What makes you. . .you."

Oh, my. Heat flamed her face. Maybe he did live as a drifter, but she wondered if he'd ever turned a young lady's head with such an uncomplicated remark, one that made a woman feel so special. Not that he'd need to do a lot of turning! Looking into his eyes, shining as blue as an evening sky in the first bloom of springtime, she sensed that Derek Burke spoke just as he felt.

She cleared her throat, trying to regain the thread to their prior conversation. "The day we met, you mentioned you have a brother. Does he live in Nevada?"

"He's in Nevada at present."

The words didn't sound happy. "Any other kin?"

"None that I plan to claim."

Now, what did that mean? Curious, she stared, noting his

pensive scowl. Rather than ask, she waited, not wanting to push him so that he withdrew again.

"As a matter of fact, I saw my brother last week," he said after a moment. "The day before I ran into you."

"He lives near here?"

"Not exactly."

When he offered no further explanation, Penny took in a deep breath for patience. Oh, he could be the most infuriating man sometimes! Recalling her resolve to keep silent, Penny waited with the hope he would continue. Her desire for information had gone beyond curiosity due to caution; now she wanted to know, simply to learn all she could about this man.

"My pa. . .passed away recently. My brother and I met up not long after in a small mining town about a day's ride from the valley where you lived."

"Silverton?"

He nodded.

Now she felt bad for her earlier irritation. "I'm sorry for your loss."

"Not necessary. I barely knew him. Last time we spent any time together, I was just a young'un, and the time we spent was scarce."

"Your brother or your pa?"

"Both. And now it's too late. I wouldn't have even come here if not for the letters we three got informing us to meet up at Pa's request."

"Three? So there's more than just you and your brother?"

Another uneasy stretch of silence passed.

"No one, really. Someone trying to pass themselves off as family," he muttered.

"Why should they do that?" She posed the question under

her breath, trying to sort out the puzzle of the history his life presented.

"Why else? She wants to interfere where she has no place."

Sensing him withdraw, she thought it wise to change the subject. "You once spoke of your mother. Tell me about her."

A slight, wistful smile tilted his lips. "She was a wise woman with faith as big as a mountain, though she was stern enough when it came to any of my shenanigans."

"You loved her."

He nodded. "I did. She'd been a schoolteacher before she married my pa, and she took to the words of the Bible just like you do."

"But you don't?"

He shrugged. "I believe there's a God, all right, was raised that way by my ma. I just don't see that He ever did all that much good for me."

A lode of pain was buried beneath his solemn words. Any rebuttal Penny might have given lodged in her throat when he turned her way and she saw the sorrow mirrored in his telling eyes.

She cleared her throat to speak. "Well now, Derek, with that I would have to disagree." At her easy use of his Christian name, his eyes flickered in surprise, followed by a faded grin and approving nod. "After all," she continued, "I have in my possession a sacred and revered book with what must amount to thousands of pages to prove the very opposite."

"That sounds like something Ma would have said."

"You did mention she was a wise woman."

He chuckled, then grew quiet, studying her face. "She would have liked you."

So many compliments in one night after a year without any

put her off balance, and she rose to her feet. "I should get busy with putting things away." She didn't miss his disappointed expression and knew a moment's surprise. Perhaps now that she'd finally gotten him to converse with her, he found he liked it. She didn't want this pleasant evening to end between them, either. Several tasks, however, awaited before she could bed down for the night.

"You knew that hidden spring was there all along, didn't you?"

His low words coming so suddenly after a lapse of quiet caused her to start. She looked his way before gathering the tins and stacking them in the empty kettle. "Aye."

"How come you didn't tell me about it?"

She hesitated before speaking. "I suppose I should have. But I figured if I mentioned it, you might think me foolish to go off searching for the springs when we have the river near."

"I wouldn't have thought that of you."

"No?" His assurance made her smile. "You called me foolish once before."

He fidgeted with his hat, which he'd pulled off. "That was before I knew you."

His sincere words hit Penny with the force of a strong wind; oddly shy, she looked away. "My da told me about finding the spring in his travels. From the manner in which he described the area, I assumed this must be the place. Have you ever bathed in a heated spring?"

"Can't say that I have."

" 'Tis a delightful experience. One of the best that I've encountered."

"So I've heard."

She shot him a quick look at his choice of words, sensing

a thread of humor woven through them. His attention had moved to the harmonica he now held in his hand.

Penny thought of her sleeping girls in the wagon but wanted to prolong her time with Derek. "Do you know any quiet tunes on that mouth organ?"

He raised his brow and looked at her. "Quiet?"

"Slow. Fit for the night."

"I might recall a couple. Ma liked that type of tune, too. Especially after a hard day's work was done. She'd often sit on the porch of an evening and watch the sunset. Said it was a shame not to enjoy the colors in the clouds that God painted to close each day."

Penny nodded, recognizing where he'd received his ability to simplify pictures into appealing words.

"Once the day ended, she had a rule that all the cares went with it. Then she got sick and needed medicine." He propped his knee up, laying his forearm across it. "That's when I left to find work and earn money to send home. I never went back, and Clay never forgave me."

"There's still time."

At her soft words, he swung his brooding gaze her way.

"Your brother isn't dead. And neither are you."

"I might as well be for all the good it'll do me. He isn't willing to forget or forgive. And now he likely never will." His jaw hardened.

She wondered at his peculiar words and what ran through his mind but decided this time she wouldn't ask. Regretting that she'd stirred up a nest of bitterness, Penny changed the subject, hoping to recapture the easy peace they'd shared. "I remember when life seemed free of all cares. As a child, the world didn't seem so harsh, and it was easy to get caught up in one's imaginings and just dream the bad away. My da was a hardworking man, but he knew how to find pleasure when life offered it, much like your ma, I expect. He taught me the reels from his homeland and an appreciation for music, though he could scarce carry a tune." She chuckled. "I miss the manner in which he would sweep me 'round the room with my small hands in his big ones."

Derek smiled in acknowledgement, seeming to relax by degrees, and she turned to resume her task of sorting and packing up the tins. Behind her, the mournful, soft notes of a familiar tune trembled in the air. She recognized it as a song her da used to play, though not as well as Derek. Busy at her task, without paying much attention to anything but her work and the sweet music, she began to hum the melody and continued for a few notes, even after the harmonica's notes abruptly ceased.

She heard Derek approach from behind. To her surprise, he laid a gentle hand atop her shoulder. She glanced at his fingers, lean and strong, then looked over her shoulder into his eyes, turning slowly as she did.

"Don't stop," he said, "you have a beautiful voice."

"Sure, and you wouldna be wantin' me to—"

"Please," he insisted, his tone soft, quelling her hoarse refusal.

She looked up into his steady blue eyes. Confidence gradually crested inside her, and she began to hum again. His question and her response suddenly seemed so natural, so fitting into this entire evening. The night belonged to a fantastic tale much like the ones that stemmed from her da's homeland.

Wrapped up in the dream, Penny felt little shock when

Derek reached for her hand that hung by her side and took it in his large one. Her voice died in her throat at Derek's first warm touch. He wrapped his long fingers around hers with care, lifting their clasped hands to the level of her shoulder. "Don't stop," he whispered again. He then cupped his other strong hand with the slightest pressure at her waist, and slowly began to circle with her, his steps agile and sure. When he began to dance with her beneath the star-tossed quilt of the black velvet night, she found a thread of the song again and resumed humming. Uncertain what to do with her free hand, she laid it against his sleeve, her fingertips pressed against his strong muscle for balance.

She'd never learned the steps to this dance and felt awkward. But Derek exercised patience, and she soon attuned to his lead, as if she'd danced with him for years. They both smiled as he swirled her over the sand and past the sagebrush in the pale ring of security cast by the light from their campfire. Feeling giddy, not remembering the last time she'd known such freedom, Penny tilted her head back and laughed low in delight.

Derek stopped so suddenly she caught her breath. His expression grew earnest, his gaze intent, as he stared at her mouth then back to her startled eyes.

"You can dance," she managed the only words that came to mind, no matter how banal or obvious. "I wouldn't have thought a drifter would know how."

His lips quirked into the slightest grin. "Ma showed me, thought I should learn." His voice seemed to come from afar, and again his gaze drifted to her mouth. "When she was young, a wealthy friend taught her. Said someday it might benefit me, knowing a waltz or two."

Penny didn't retreat as he unclasped his hand from hers and moved his finger beneath her chin, tilting it up. "And she gave you her love for music," she whispered, glancing at his mouth as he lowered his head.

"Yeah. . .I'm beholden to her for that."

When his lips touched hers, the caress came as soft as a breath. Warm and gentle, yet so powerful she felt she might be knocked off her feet. Her pounding heart rivaled the quiet, tender moment, and she tightened her fingers against his arm to remain upright and steady.

When he pulled away, no apology for his unexpected act entered his eyes. Nor did she want one. They stared at each other breathless seconds before she lifted her face to receive his second kiss.

The sound of the girls' soft laughter reached Penny's ears. Stunned, she broke away from Derek as though he'd scalded her. She took a step back, her hand covering her bosom, though nothing would calm her racing heart. She glanced toward the wagon, as did he. Both Olivia and Christa peeked at them from around the canvas, giggling behind their hands.

❧

"I—I should go and tend to them," Penny stammered, her dark eyes huge in her flushed face.

Derek nodded. "It's getting late. I'll finish up here."

"You?"

"I learned how to pack a dish or two, being a drifter and all."

With the way she winced before she nodded her thanks and gave a weak smile, he wished he could retrieve his ill-thought-out words. They sounded like a reminder of his preference to remain a loner. And that was what he did want, wasn't it? Not to get involved with a woman? Not to put down roots or saddle himself with further responsibilities?

As he watched Penny hurry to the wagon, Derek tried to forget the feel of her in his arms. He realized he'd been foolish to follow through with his desire to kiss her. Her inborn strength amazed him, solid and rare like a precious metal; something most men sought after. While at other times her self-determination and stubbornness provoked him. Yet she was all a woman should be, too. Soft and warm. Gentle and caring. All those traits wrapped into one bundle were reason enough to not kiss her. She was getting under his skin in a way no other woman ever had.

When he'd heard her quiet words concerning her da and seen the sweet sadness in her eyes at the memories, that had been bad enough, striking in him a chord of similar regret. But once she began humming along with Derek's tune, her pleasing voice, both lyrical and wistful, touched him in a way that made him want to help her forget the pain and recall all the joy.

And that was dangerous.

He'd spent more than half his life trying to be the man of the family and fill the empty shoes his pa left behind—both in action and in fact. They'd struggled a great deal after his father left to seek his fortune, and Derek had needed to wear his pa's huge castoff boots since they'd had no money to buy new ones. He'd despised each step he took in the hard, roughened leather, not wanting to be anything like their former owner. Realizing his pa had taken his life journey in the ill-fitting boots made the fourteen-year-old Derek hate him all the more.

The first thing he'd done when he left home and earned enough money was buy himself a new pair of boots. Other than necessities, the rest of the money went to his ma and Clay. He'd done more than his share in taking care of family and had received little gratitude for his sacrifice; was it so wrong that he now wished to take care of himself and realize his own dreams?

With the profits from the mine, he'd thought about claiming a parcel of land and starting a ranch. He'd had some experience as a cowboy a few years back, one of many jobs he'd taken on. Since then, the idea of ranch life had found a comfortable home in his head. When he got the itch to travel and felt too settled in, a roundup always loomed on the horizon. Yet a successful rancher needed a wife, or so he'd been led to believe by the man who'd hired him—a gracious, well-mannered woman to entertain his guests, with the inborn strength to handle the difficulties that came with life on a ranch. A woman with the fortitude to give him sons. But Derek wouldn't mind a few strong daughters, either.

His gaze went to the wagon, where he could see Penny's silhouette through the canvas. He watched the shadow of her arms move as she braided her hair.

A woman like Penny. . .he couldn't go wrong there.

Derek shook his head at the crazy rabbit trail his mind had taken. One brief kiss, and he planned a future with her as his wife?

"What's the matter with me?" he muttered as he finished the few tasks she'd left undone. He couldn't afford such thoughts, not now. Not when he was so close to finding his fortune. The claim must come first; nothing could take priority over that.

Derek passed a night of fitful sleep. Dreams of himself and Clay as youngsters troubled his mind, with Penny suddenly standing off to the side, beckoning to Derek, her brown eyes beseeching—and he awoke with a start. The sky was still dark, the moon hidden behind a hill. After failing to get comfortable, Derek sat up to feed the burning embers of the fire. He grabbed the coffeepot from the hot, white ashes, finding it near empty. If the coffee beans weren't kept in the wagon, he would start a pot to brew. He sure could use more than one cup right now; he felt so tense.

A black-blue haze soon filmed the land with the approach of sunup, and a dark shape materialized by the wagon, detaching itself from the back. Derek recognized Christa, but before he could call to her, she scampered for the same hill her ma had visited the previous day.

"Christa! Come back here!" His quiet but firm shout didn't do a bit of good. She either ignored him or didn't hear, and Derek set down the coffeepot with a muttered oath.

Grabbing his gun belt, he took off after her. Too many dangers lurked beyond those rocks, and he wasn't about to wait for her safe return.

ten

Penny woke at the same time she always did, just before sunup, as the forerunner to daybreak painted the hills and land in a mist of dusky blue. To her alarm, she noticed both girls' spots empty in the wagon bed and hurried to climb down. During this journey, she had slept in her moccasins and dress, considering the discomfort necessary in the event she might have to rush from the wagon for whatever reason.

Like now.

"Morning, Mama!" Christa's cheerful voice greeted her. She hopped up from where she sat with her cornhusk doll and ran to Penny, throwing her arms around her, doll and all.

"Good morning." Still disconcerted by the scare but at the same time relieved all was well, Penny noticed Olivia feeding bits of sagebrush to the fire. Their guide was nowhere in sight. "Where's Mr. Burke?"

Christa craned her head to look up at Penny. "He went behind that hill. Can we have a breakfast like dinner was?"

Surprised, Penny glanced at the shadowed hill in curiosity before returning her gaze to her daughter. "Did he say when he'd be back?"

Christa shook her head. "I wanted to see the spring, but he made me come back here."

"Made you come back. . ." Penny assumed a stern countenance as she pieced the meaning of her daughter's explanation together. "Christabel Louise! Did you go look for the hidden pool without me?"

A guilty expression filled the girl's dark eyes, and she bowed her head. "You said it wasn't far. I thought it might make my stomach feel better. And I *had* to go."

Penny shook her head. Christa's late-night ventures to tend to nature's callings often led her down trails that sparked her childish curiosity.

"You know you're not supposed to wander off from the wagon. I said you should wait till dawn when I would take both you and Olivia to the spring."

"Can we go now?"

"No!" She blurted her answer, recalling the previous day's incident when Derek sought her out. Seeing Christa's confusion, she collected herself. "Not till after Mr. Burke returns. If he is taking advantage of the hot springs, I have no wish to disturb him."

Penny collected the items needed to make breakfast. First, she boiled water to start coffee, then ground a handful of beans and dumped them into the pot. "What are you so glum about?" She shifted her attention to her eldest who'd said nary a word nor showed the slightest amount of cheer.

Olivia continued to stare into the fire. "I don't see why we always have to bathe in the river or anywhere else besides. Why not just stay dirty?"

"Olivia! What a question!"

"Being clean didn't make nobody else like us. And I'll bet Mr. Burke doesn't care." She looked up at Penny. "What if the new people don't like us, either?"

"What new people?" Penny wrinkled her brow at her daughter's solemn question.

"In Carson City. What if they don't want nothin' to do with

us, either? I'll bet most of 'em are miners, just like back home."

Cutting words, hopelessly aired; words that Penny had avoided even in thought from the moment she'd devised this plan to go farther west. They twisted like brambles around her heart, piercing her with pain surely only a mother could feel; the thorns, her child's sorrow.

"Maybe we should've just stayed there," Olivia added quietly.

Penny refused to succumb. From experience she knew the best solution was to snap her daughter from her doldrums. "Now then, Olivia Meredith, do you mind telling me what put such a fool notion into your head?"

Her eldest let out a dismal sigh and flicked the band of her slingshot a few times. "I was just thinking about that story we read in the Bible yesterday, about them lepers and how nobody wanted them around."

"Those lepers. And the lepers were people who had a disease others could catch. It makes sense that people in the city wouldn't want them around so as to protect their own. Just like I protect you and Christa, and Mr. Burke protects all of us."

"But Jesus healed them and made them whole again, didn't He? That's what you read. But we'll always be the same, won't we, Mama? What happened to those lepers isn't much different than the way them—those miners treated us. But Jesus made it so people could like them. Do you think He'd do the same for us if I asked Him to in my prayers?"

Oh, if she could take all her girls' heartache so they'd never again have to suffer the ignorance of men! Penny counted to three under her breath and composed a calm response.

"Well now, Olivia, there's not a blessed thing wrong with

either of my girls. Och, and it's a good thing to pray and ask God for those things that you know would please Him as well. Asking Him to make you more likeable isn't a bad thing. But you and Christa are perfect just as God made you. As for those fool miners, not everyone is so crude or so cruel. Your dear papa was a kind man who had not an ounce of prejudice in him. Your grandda was the same. And your great-grandfather, and Mr. Burke. . ." That she should feel her cheeks flush at the mere mention of his name made her flounder. "Well now. He's proven to be a man of admirable qualities. Most trustworthy." Again she busied herself, briskly stirring flour and water in a bowl and pouring the mixture into her iron spider, which she set over the low flames.

"You like Mr. Burke, don't you, Mama?"

How to answer that! "Aye. I would imagine everyone who meets him recognizes the good in him. It's easy to appreciate a man like that."

"You plan on marryin' him?"

Penny froze. Eyes going wide, she swung her head around to stare at her daughter.

"You kissed him." Olivia shot a sly grin her mother's way and Christa giggled. "I was just wondering." With the prongs of her slingshot, Olivia began to trace lines through the sandy topsoil. "'Cause I wouldn't mind if you did. He's not Papa, but I like him. And he plays the harmonica real good. He said he'd teach me what he knows."

"I like him, too!" Christa added with enthusiasm.

Penny felt her face warm again. A better question to ask, whatever had gotten into her head? She could scarce believe she'd allowed him the liberty. But last evening she hadn't thought much at all. The sweet music gently rolling through the canyon had reminded her of happier days, while the cool night refreshed her and the canopy of twinkling stars, with the moon winking at them from beyond the clouds had set her imagination soaring. When he'd taken her in his arms in what he called a waltz, it had seemed quite right, and she hadn't thought to deny him. Nor had she wanted to deny him the kiss. Two kisses. . .

He's a drifter who wants nothing to do with marriage, her pesky thoughts reminded. *Nor does he seem to really serve God.*

"Mama?"

Snapped out of her musings, Penny returned her attention to her eldest daughter.

"You really think we'll have a better life in Carson City?"

"Ye canna spend a lifetime runnin' from your problems, Penelope MacPhearson." Penny inhaled a swift breath as her da's old admonition ran through her head, gentle words of firm counsel he'd given when as a small girl she'd fled from the mocking, hurtful words of children at the trading post to find a place to hide. *"Ye'll spend a lifetime runnin' in circles, never t' find the end of the road ye think will take ye t' happiness—and that be the gospel truth, lass. True happiness can only be found in here."* He'd patted his chest. *"With the good Laird dwellin' within. And dinnae be forgettin' I spoke so."*

"I think," she started and cleared her throat from the catch that made her words waver. "We Crawders are strong enough to bloom and survive wherever we're planted."

Olivia looked confused. "Then why did we leave the valley? I liked it there. Well, except for those evil miners. But we had good times, too, especially when Papa was alive and the miners left us alone."

"Change can be a good thing. We'll have good times again."

Penny smiled, trying to make light of her words though the heaviness inside refused to budge. "We have that grand thirst for adventure in our blood that came from your grandda and your great-grandmother Kimama. Her tribe was nomadic, and many, many days ago, they wandered over this great land."

Olivia's eyes shone, wistful. "Will you tell us their stories again? And about their lives among the Shoshone?"

"Later perhaps. First we must have our daily reading." Derek had taken to joining them when she read from the Holy Book, and she didn't want him to miss the opportunity.

"It might help me feel more keen on the idea of living in Carson City," Olivia said simply, her impish grin somehow managing to appear guileless.

Penny recognized a bit of innocent manipulation on her daughter's part and debated whether she should give her a gentle scolding or fulfill her hopeful request. She loved passing down the stories her da and mother had told her and decided that this morning, she would overlook the bit of skillful artifice on Olivia's part. She thought back to a story her daughter always enjoyed, that of her da's first encounter with the Shoshone, when he'd returned to a trap he'd laid to find the woman who would become his wife, her ankle caught in his noose.

"Mama." Christa came up beside her, her voice wavering in fear, and clutched Penny's shoulder tight. Her wide eyes focused on the trail from which they'd come.

Penny looked over her shoulder to see two men on horse-back, not fifty feet distant and headed their way.

"Olivia," she said calmly as she rose from her crouch and slipped a protective arm around Christa's shoulders. "Get the shotgun from the wagon and bring it to me."

Olivia threw a look in the direction of the men, and her face lost color. She shot up from the ground in a flurry, running to the wagon while Penny turned around with Christa. She took a step forward, keeping her child well behind her.

As the men drew near, she noticed one held a rifle across his saddle. Both wore guns at their hips. Their clothes were shabby, and dark, days-old beards whiskered their faces. Their hair hung long and straggly about their shoulders. These men didn't appear to be simple miners, and the word *outlaws* flashed across her mind.

She heard Olivia's running steps behind her, but before Penny could turn to retrieve her shotgun, the man minus the rifle hunched over, one hand going to the saddle horn, the other to his handgun.

"I wouldn't do that if I was you," he growled in a mock pleasant manner as he withdrew his gun from his holster in a flash of silver. His sorrel picked up pace until scant distance separated them. "Put the gun down, Injun gal, 'less you want a bullet through your head."

The other rider brought his gray to the other side, closing them in.

"Put the gun down, Livvie." Penny kept her voice firm, masking her fear. She wouldn't let these scoundrels frighten her into submission, but at the same time, she would do anything to protect her children. *God help us.*

The leader flicked his hat up from his brow with the hand holding the gun, taking time to eye Penny from the top of her braided hair to her moccasin-clad feet. "Well, now, what've we got here, Jonesy," he said in an aside to his partner. "An Injun squaw, I reckon. A right pretty one, too, and ripe for the picking."

"Yeah," the second man also leered her way. "Maybe we should rest here a spell, Amos."

Penny kept her silence, ready to fight them, biting and clawing if she must. She glanced at the iron spider in front of her, hot from the fire, and wondered if she could move quick enough to do damage with it.

As though he read her mind, the leader dismounted, swaggering toward Penny. "First, we'll take some of that coffee I smell brewin'. And whatever breakfast you can cook up. Once we fill our bellies, we can get to know one another better." He stroked the muzzle of his cold gun from the corner of her mouth to her cheek, then followed it with the back of his coarse hand. She flinched at his touch, knocking his arm away.

He guffawed, seeming both surprised and amused. "So, you got fire in you! But too fair a skin and light-colored eyes for a full-blooded Injun; and your hair's got red in it, too." As he spoke the last, he fondled one of her long braids, taking it in his meaty paw. "I reckon you must have some white man's blood in there. . .but you're still nothing but a squaw."

She recoiled at his vicious words. He gripped the plait hard, yanking it toward him so that her scalp burned and she fought for balance. Behind her, Christa began to cry softly.

A shot rang out of nowhere, echoing through the canyon. The lecher's hat flew to the dirt. Startled, he released her braid.

"Keep your hands off her, or the next bullet will go through your head," Derek called out. Relief made Penny dizzy, and she struggled to remain standing.

The two outlaws frantically looked around—at the wagon, at the hills on both sides. Derek was nowhere in sight. The second man still on horseback swiftly moved to train his rifle on Penny. Before he could complete the act, another shot had his hat flying.

"If you pull a stunt like that again, next time my aim centers on your middle," Derek shouted. "Though I doubt you have a heart to put a bullet through. Throw down your guns—both of you. Then get back on your horse, nice and slow, and head back the way you came. If either of you comes near them again, two busted hats will be the least of your worries."

The man called Jonesy threw down his guns. The leader delivered a hateful glare to the hill in the opposite direction that Penny thought Derek's voice came from. Letting his gun drop, he glanced at her in disgust and turned toward his horse.

"That goes for the other one, too."

At Derek's order, the man grimaced and pulled the second pistol from his holster, letting it drop next to the other. The leader took a few steps, scooped up his hat from the dirt, and strode to his horse. He faced his saddle as though he would mount up. Instead, his hands went to the butt of the rifle she now noticed sticking out from the side.

Before Penny could call out a warning, Derek emerged from a waist-high grouping of rocks near the wagon, both his pistols aimed at the men who swung their focus his way.

The leader snapped his rifle from its leather scabbard and brought it up fast. Two more shots rang out, and Christa screamed.

eleven

The leader swore and grabbed his arm. Bright red spread across his blue sleeve.

"I said drop your guns," Derek reminded, his voice calm but cold as flint. "That means all of them."

Derek continued his easy stride toward camp; in a lightning swift arc, he spun both his guns by the trigger loops with his index fingers. As they completed their rotation, he again grabbed them by their handles and aimed one at each man. "You don't want to try me."

The desperado he'd nicked in the arm spewed a string of vulgar words at Derek that contained mention of him being a "no-good Injun lover." Out of the corner of his eye, he noticed Penny clap her hands over Christa's ears at the first onslaught.

"That's no way to talk in the presence of a lady or her girls," Derek said, keeping his voice still though his blood boiled. "I recommend you just do as I say; then the both of you ride on out of here before I really get upset and teach you a lesson."

With a final glare, the leader dropped his rifle to the ground and mounted his horse with some difficulty. Both outlaws turned their horses east and galloped away.

Derek waited a moment before holstering his guns. Despite his legs feeling shaky, as though sand filtered through his knees, he walked toward Penny, gratified to see her safe. She held both her girls close. The muscles of her slender jaw stretched taut, and he reconsidered laying his hand upon her shoulder, though what he would have really liked to do was pull her into his arms and hold her close to his heart. It had near stopped beating when he'd returned from his visit to the springs and seen that despicable snake fondle her.

"Are you—" he began.

"I'm all right," she said before he could finish his concerned query. "I should have known better than to leave my shotgun in the wagon. I usually have it within reach at all times. What was I thinking?"

Both girls turned their faces up to look at their mother. By the frowns etched in their foreheads, he saw that they also worried about their ma and the high pitch in her usually quiet voice.

"You ought not blame yourself," Derek insisted.

Before he could say more, she speared him with a glance that silenced him. "I need to finish breakfast." She retreated from all of them toward the three-legged skillet sitting over the fire. The three watched as her hands gripped her folded arms and she hugged herself, staring down at the spider. The girls swung their confused gazes to Derek as if seeking direction.

"Livvie, why don't you take Christa to the wagon and show her that harmonica of yours. Or maybe there's something else you can do before we break camp, some chores your ma has you do of a morning?"

"Okay." She glanced at her ma, then at Derek, and took her sister's hand. "Come along, Christa."

Christa looked up at Derek. "You gonna take care of our ma, Mr. Burke?"

The gentle smile he gave at her soft, plaintive words didn't release the fear from her eyes. "Your ma will be fine. I'll talk to her."

"I'm glad you'll be with us in Carson City so no bad men can hurt us anymore."

Before he could correct Christa's somber words that he would remain with their family, she turned and walked to the wagon with Olivia. Someone needed to set things straight; he had no idea how the girls had gotten it into their heads that he would stay with them. But there was time to sort that out later.

Again he watched Penny, who stood with her rigid back toward him. First, he supposed he should try and talk to her. He wished he had better experience with such a thing but felt out of his depth, like the time years ago when a riverbank he'd crossed had suddenly given way and swirling water had closed over his head.

Derek moved to stand at her elbow, but she paid him no mind. She dumped out the charred mess of a johnnycake and poured more of the runny mix from the bowl into the spider. Her actions came jerky, as if her bones weren't fused right.

He cleared his throat. "About what just happened—"

"I'll try to hurry breakfast. I know you're hungry." Still she didn't look at him. Her tone sounded unnatural, forced. "And I promised the girls I'd take them to the spring before we leave. But I don't have to do that if you'd rather get a quick start."

"You don't have to hurry. Take your time."

"Nonsense." She snatched a tin mug from the crate of utensils. "Can I pour you some coffee while you wait? I know a man likes his coffee of a morning. My husband and da did, and I imagine you're no different."

Before she could grab the coffeepot from the fire, he gently grasped her forearms and turned her toward him. "Did he hurt you?"

"No." She evaded his gaze. "I don't want to talk about it."

"I understand that, Penny. But you're scaring your girls." He watched her dart a glance to the wagon. Both Olivia and Christa had withdrawn behind the canvas and now peeked around it. "You can't blame yourself for what happened, if that's what you're doing," he said again.

"I can." She pierced him with her gaze, keeping her voice low. "And I do. I'm their mother. Things could have ended far worse had you not come along. I should have known better, to have my gun nearby at all times—"

"And now you have eight, including mine," he joked, hoping to draw her from her foul mood and get her at least to crack a smile. "You really are a woman with her own fort."

She looked at the piles of discarded weapons. "It seems wrong to take them, somehow."

"Would you rather I had let those men remain armed and given them good reason to sneak up on us to seek their idea of a reckoning?"

"No, of course not. I just. . ." She bit the edge of her lower lip. "Do you suppose it's all right? They don't belong to us."

"The snakes and lizards don't have use for them. Only other choice would be to let them bake in the heat, which would lead to their ruin. If they can be used to protect you and your girls instead of for a crime, which I'm sure those scoundrels used them for, then I don't see the problem. I've had the misfortune of meeting up with that sort before; likely those men stole the guns off their victims."

"I see your point." She continued staring at the guns. "I suppose it would be all right then, if we give them over to the sheriff in Carson City once we arrive. Or come to a town before that with a lawman. That way it wouldn't really seem like we're taking what isn't ours, only doing our civic duty by delivering the guns into safekeeping."

"Fair enough."

She smoothed her hands down the front of her skirt, casting him a rueful glance. "Thank you for. . .everything. I should have said that first."

"Only doing what you hired me to do."

"No, you've done so much more." For the first time, she smiled, and though it came strained, she seemed to have again found that inner strength he so admired.

⁂

After supper, with the canyon behind them and what she hoped were many more miles between them and their attackers, Penny sat near the fire. The breeze felt almost pleasant, not the hot wind of the afternoon. Enough daylight remained, and the focused work of sewing seed beads onto buckskin helped soothe her nerves.

With slow care, she stitched a design onto one of the flaps of five pouches she'd brought to sell at the trading post. She'd been jumpy ever since the morning's encounter. The events had rattled her composure, and she'd waited to read their daily chapter at the noon break when she felt calm again, with no further thought that she might break down and cry if she tried.

Now, with the day well behind them, she finally began to relax.

Olivia perched at the edge of the wagon, swinging her legs and repeatedly blowing the notes to a short tune Derek had taught her, as she'd done since she finished her meal. Grateful that the warbling from the harmonica had grown steadier, Penny glanced up and across the fire at Derek, appreciating the manner in which his hair blew back from his face. He'd shed his hat and sat near Christa, who peppered him with questions concerning the noon reading as she'd been doing since he poured his first cup of coffee.

"You think King Solomon was wise?" Christa asked, and Penny again glanced up from her work. Her daughter's eyes glowed with curiosity as she regarded Derek.

"I imagine so." He took the last swig of his second cup of coffee, tipping the tin back to drain it.

"But why would he tell the women he was going to cut the baby in half? Isn't it bad to kill, no matter what? And that was just a wee baby."

"Well now, he didn't use his sword, did he?"

"No. . . ," Christa trailed off. "But he might have."

"I think he just wanted to get those ladies thinking. He knew the woman who really loved the child would never let it die. And that would be the real mama."

"But she almost gave her baby away." Christa wrinkled her brow, hard at thought. "So she must not have loved it much if she'd give it away to the other woman. Isn't that so?"

Derek seemed stymied for an answer, and Penny hid a smile, sensing he was flummoxed by her girl's insistent questions.

"Christa," she said under her breath, her attention never straying from the needle as she carefully stitched the cobalt beadwork in a triangle pattern. "Moses's mother did much the same. Remember when I read his story? And she loved her son very much. Fact is, sometimes a mother must make hard choices for the best interest of her child. And sometimes mothers—anyone really—must give up those things they want most in the world to help their family or keep them together. I expect God blessed both women for their sacrifice and their willingness to let go, all for the sake of their children. Family is all that any of us have, really; all that God gave us. Family will stand beside us and love us till our dying breaths. The good Lord intended it that way, that no one should be alone."

She looked up to catch Derek's gaze on her and wondered what put such a somber look in his eyes, then recalled his words about his own family. She hadn't intended to go on so but got carried away in the opportunity to teach her daughter a worthy lesson.

"But, Mama, King Solomon might have killed that baby if its mama hadn't given it up." Christa's brow clouded. "Do you think he would've killed it, Mr. Burke?"

"I think Solomon was a fair man. I don't think he would have done wrong, since everyone had such a high opinion of him."

"Have you ever killed anyone?"

Derek jerked his head in surprise, and Penny sensed his unease as he looked into the fire.

"Christa, that's enough." She looked over the pouch at her daughter.

Christa let out a sigh. "Sorry, Mama. Sorry, Mr. Burke." She stood to her feet. "Can I go lie down now?"

Surprised that she didn't have to instruct her child to go to bed, Penny peered at her face, noticing it seemed a little more drawn than before. "Aren't you feeling well? Did those sagebrush leaves that I gave you help?"

Christa pulled a face. "They taste icky."

"That's no reason not to chew them. Not everything that's good for you goes down sweet."

"Okay." Christa sighed, hugging her doll close.

"Tell Olivia it's her bedtime, too."

Christa took a few steps, then looked back at Derek. "I think you're a fair man, Mr. Burke. Mama said so. So I'm sure if you killed someone, or almost did, God'll understand."

"It's never okay to kill, Christa," Derek said quietly. "But sometimes, in defense, a man isn't given much choice." He looked up at Christa. "I came close when I met up with some cattle rustlers once, but no, I've never killed a man. Not to my knowledge."

"You were a cowboy?" Interest lit Christa's eyes. "On a ranch? Is that where you learned to shoot so good? And to spin your guns like you did?"

"Christa . . . ," Penny cautioned her errant child.

Derek chuckled, though it sounded tight. "You'd be surprised what a man does to pass the time when he's alone, like learning fancy tricks with his guns. I had a friend teach me a few things, too, before he became a sheriff. I reckon I've been a number of things, and yeah, a cowboy was one of them. I'll tell you about it sometime. But you should obey your ma now."

Christa nodded without another word and left for the wagon.

"So you do have friends somewhere?" Penny inquired with a smile.

"A few." His tone didn't share her amusement at her less than subtle prod, and she noticed that he watched Christa's retreat with sober eyes. "Has she always been sickly? Ever since I joined up with you, she seems to lose more strength each day."

Uneasy, Penny returned her attention to her beadwork. "I nearly lost her two years after she was born. She got sick with a fever that winter and has never been the same since." When he remained silent, she glanced up. His brows had pulled together in a worried frown. "Something else troubling you, Derek?"

He took in a deep breath and let it out slowly. "I didn't know that when I agreed to be your guide." Penny felt as if a fist grabbed her heart at the gravity in his eyes. "I can't take you any farther without you knowing what we're up against."

"Up against?" Dread made it difficult to breathe.

"The river ends in a sink. Beyond that lies nothing but forty miles of desert. No water. No shade. No feed for the livestock. Alkali flats as far as the eye can see and loose sand that buries wagon wheels and makes travel near impossible. The sun reflects off the land and hills so hot you feel as if your eyes are burned and you're being baked alive. Men much stronger than Christa haven't made it across."

Horrified, Penny stared, putting into words what he didn't say. "You're telling me that you don't think my little girl can survive the journey."

She could see how difficult it was to answer by the way he averted his eyes and shifted his hat a bit where it sat propped on his knee. "Frankly, yes. That's what I'm saying."

"What about Virginia City?" She would have preferred Carson City, to try to find her brother-in-law, but now grabbed at any alternative. "Is that safer? We could go there instead."

He looked at her. "We would need to cross the same desert."

His quiet words, his grave expression sent her mind into a spin, and she rose to her feet. "I—I have to go. To think things through. I'll speak with you further about this in the morning."

He nodded and again stared into the fire.

Barely able to contain the whirlwind of her emotions, Penny headed for the wagon.

How. . .how could a few words spoken cause everything to go so wrong? Cause her long-held dreams to vanish so abruptly? All her bright hopes crashed around her like fallen sparrows struck by a hunter's merciless bullets. Why had her da never told her about that particular stretch of desert and the alkali flats? She knew he'd been as far as Virginia City; if he knew, why hadn't he said anything? Had he been anxious he might frighten his little girl with distressing accounts unlike the inspiring tales he'd told? The emigrants she'd met must not have known what they would come up against to speak of it, but Penny should have. She should have asked Derek what the entire journey was like in advance. She'd been so sure she could do this, that it was the right thing to do! To leave her homestead and follow Derek to Carson City.

There had to be some way.

She climbed into the back of the wagon and looked upon the wan face of her youngest, now fast asleep. Her heart whispered the truth, echoing his cautions. Christa was too weak to survive days in a situation such as Derek had described, one that would test the mettle of the strongest men.

"Mama?" Olivia whispered. "Is everything okay? Why are you crying?"

Penny hadn't realized she was and lifted her hand to swipe at her cheek, only just realizing she still carried the pouch with thread and needle attached. She'd left the pouch of seed beads open near the fire.

"Everything is fine. Go back to sleep." She failed to keep the tremor from her voice and left the wagon, not wanting Olivia to see her distress.

As she again quietly approached the fire, she watched Derek pull some papers apart to spread on the ground, what looked like the same papers she'd seen him stare at on a previous night. He weighted one corner of the first with a rock, but before he could do the same with the second, he caught notice of her and jerked his head around. The breeze caught the other two slips of paper. He scrambled to catch one. The third flew toward her, plastering itself against her fringed hem and moccasins.

"Wait!" he called out at the same time she bent to grasp the paper and lift it to her eyes. Her finger ran along the edge as she did, and she felt the sting of a cut.

A map. The papers were a map—all one map since the symbols ran off the edge and one of the sketches was half there. But not a map torn in parts from being worn. . .the sharp edge that cut her finger had been sheared. All the sides were straight, not ragged. Three parts. One map. . .with a black, bold X in the upper left corner. A treasure map. *Three* parts. . .three. . .

Penny blinked as awareness dawned, slow and bright and painful. She gaped at Derek. The wary manner in which he regarded her, the guilt in his expression told the truth.

"You took these from your siblings?" she whispered in disbelief, making a guess while hoping it wasn't true.

His eyes grew hard. "I took what belonged to me."

"Belonged to you?" She glanced at the paper in her hands, memory of other conversations clicking inside her mind. "This was your pa's, wasn't it? This map. He did this. You said he went out looking for silver and recently died. . . ."

"Penny, give me the map." Derek rose from his place by the fire, reaching for it, but she took a step back, still thinking, remembering all past conversations when she'd finally gotten him to open up. She had kept all he shared about himself locked inside her heart, yearning to know everything about him, to know him. Now those words brought only torment.

"You met up with your brother in Silverton after years of being apart. You said you two didn't get along. You said you doubted he'd ever forgive you now. And the woman. . ." She lifted eyes unfocused with tears to him and blinked them away. "Your own flesh and blood that you will not claim. You dinnae want her to have a thing, so you took the law into your own hands and took the maps for selfish gain."

"I only have her word she's kin!" Derek shot back, his voice just as low. "Pa was wrong to do what he did—in all he did. He was an ornery cuss who enjoyed twisting the knife and gave no regard to his family. Or what happened to them."

"And you do?" She regarded him with disbelief, her heart feeling as if it, too, had been stabbed. "I trusted you. Trusted you with my girls. But you're no better than those miners who stole from me. You're a thief, just like them. Only worse. You stole from your own kin."

He winced, as if feeling the slash of her words. "You don't understand, Penny. I'm the one who took care of my family for years, toiling at jobs when I was barely old enough to grow whiskers. Sending money home so Ma would have medicine, so they'd both have food and clothes. I'm the eldest and should inherit all of the mine Pa left—if he left anything and it's not all some cruel joke."

"It would serve you right if it was!" She struggled to keep a tight rein on her anger; regardless, it burst forth. "You have a wicked idea of what's right and wrong! Who are you, Derek Burke, to decide what should belong to any man if another man gave of his own possessions in his dying wish? It's not your place. The good Lord above left His throne to save sinful men, and once He died and rose and reclaimed it, He aimed to give all His good things to all His children, not just one. How would you feel if someone stole your blessings, the blessings God intended for you?"

"You don't know what you're talking about," he muttered.

"No. For the first time, everything is clear. I've had men steal from me my entire life. My goods. My pride. My safety. And I won't let it happen again, not if I can do something to stop it." She squared her shoulders, which felt weighted down by sorrow. "This is where we part ways."

Surprise lit his eyes. "I would never harm you or your girls. You should know that by now. I'm not a thief!"

"You took from your own kind, your family." Penny shook her head slowly in pained disbelief. "And you can't even see the wrong in what you've done. If you would steal from blood kin, then how can I be trustin' you with what's mine?" Each thought spoken yielded such pain she found it difficult to breathe, to continue. She knew she had to leave him before she gave in to more tears. "I'll expect you gone in the morning when there's light enough to find your way."

Before he could reply, she crumpled the paper in her hands and threw it at him. "And here be the remainder of your fine legacy!" It bounced off his shoulder, landing at the edge of the fire. "A loner's life is all you deserve, Derek Burke."

He scrambled to save the paper, beating out the flame that curled one blackened edge.

His final act twisted the knife she felt as though he'd plunged into her back. Unable to look at him further, Penny made a fast pace back to the wagon.

❧

Derek didn't wait until morning.

His temper just as fierce as Penny's, he made quick work of saddling his bay and rode out of camp without a backward glance. The moon hadn't yet reached its fullness, but it shed enough light to continue west.

He rode half the night, muttering harsh remarks under his breath about the nerve of that woman. She'd had no right to say all she did without having lived his life. She couldn't know how callous his father had been, how resentful Clay had become. How angry and hurt Derek was to face even more proof of his father's betrayal to his wife and sons—a half sister. But that wasn't what bothered him so. That Penny's scornful words had taken seed in the soft soil of the growing ache inside him, cultivated by the guilt he daily battled—that was what angered him now.

"She had no right," he muttered. "She doesn't know."

At last, his weariness overtook his irritation, and Derek stopped for the night. Without bothering to gather branches from a nearby bush to light a fire, he slipped into his bedroll. His last image before sleep claimed him was the remembrance of the anger in Penny's wounded, dark eyes.

twelve

Penny slapped the blanket of hides over herself, tucking the edges in with unnecessarily harsh pats, struggling to understand how Derek could hoodwink his own kin. The revelation coming so soon after her plans for Carson City fell apart had made her furious, unable to restrain the words she'd hurled at him.

She was still furious.

She closed her eyes, but her thoughts remained active. Weary but unable to sleep, she rolled over as best she could in the tight space, wondering how she might have felt had her da done the same—left her mother and her and sired a child by another woman. She'd been blessed to know a family's unreserved love, but not everyone had that honor. Even raised within the circle of such love, she still possessed shortcomings she tried hard to overcome.

Her thoughts added to her sorrow, taking her into her dreams. Dreams of home. Of her girls. Of Derek.

Penny awoke with a start and a sense of dread. Darkness still colored the canvas surrounding her; she figured she'd been asleep for little more than an hour. A quick check showed that her girls lay deep in slumber, their breathing slow and steady. Knowledge that Christa was too weak to finish the journey stirred up the lingering ache inside Penny's heart. No trek to whatever better life beckoned was worth the possible sacrifice of her child.

She sat up, knowing what she must do.

Derek had proven himself as nothing but trustworthy. He'd given in to her insistence and manipulations to be their guide and had saved their lives—twice. If he'd wanted to steal from her, he'd had plenty of opportunity to do so and ride away as they slept. Instead, he'd remained with them and done all he could to guarantee their comfort and safety.

He'd been wrong to take the maps; nothing could convince her otherwise. But didn't everyone struggle with flaws of one type or another? She wished now she'd been more patient once she'd discovered his secret. She'd seen the shame spread across his features when she'd looked at the map and the hopeful appeal in his eyes when he first regarded her, as if her opinion really mattered. It was absurd, really. She had forever been urging him to talk; when he'd done so, she wouldn't listen to what he had to say.

The sun had yet to rise; she could still stop him. Apologize. Offer to listen if he would again open up and trust her. And this time, if she did offer advice to his quandaries, she would do so with gentleness and a quiet voice as her ma had done for her. Having decided, Penny scrambled down from the wagon, her hand clutching the cover for balance.

The moon's glow revealed the campsite, the shadowed clumps of sagebrush against the pale hills, the nearby river glowing nearly white, reflecting the moon. She stopped and blinked in disbelief. Derek's horse and bedroll were gone. He hadn't waited for daybreak to leave camp.

Despairing of ever seeing him again, Penny dropped her forehead to the stiff canvas. How much more pain could a heart withstand? For the first time, she realized how empty everything seemed without him there and how much she would miss his presence. For the first time, it occurred to her: She loved him.

Turning the blame on herself, she grimaced, bunching the canvas tighter in her fist. What right did she have to judge him for his treatment of his family? She, who could not grant the God-commanded absolution to strangers for stealing her goods throughout the past several months, condemned a man who blamed his kin for injustices that stretched out over the years.

The hypocrisy of her actions rankled, making her sick.

"Why is it so difficult for me? Why can't I let things go like Mother did? And Da? I don't want to feel this way. I despise feeling this way." It gave her no comfort to hold on to the old pain and bitterness, but Penny had no idea how to let go.

ॐ

Derek groaned at the pricks of something sharp along his face and neck. He opened burning eyes to the rising sun, realizing that at some point during the night his hat had fallen away from shielding his face. Swatting at the swarm of black, biting flies, he rolled over. Within several feet of his bedroll, partially covered by greasewood, lay what little remained of the carcass of a small animal. Dead more than a day, judging by the look of the bones. Likely a coyote's kill.

The memory of what had brought him to this place made him scowl. She'd had no right, but he was also angry with himself. He should have never left, even if Penny had demanded it, but he hadn't thought clearly at the time. He supposed he'd given those outlaws a good idea of what would befall them if they returned, but that didn't ease his fears of what could happen to her.

Sitting up, he noticed his horse was missing.

"What the. . . ?"

He shot out of his bedroll so fast he got his legs twined in the cloth and stumbled to a stand. Miles of sagebrush, greasewood, river, and hills—as far as the eye could see.

But no bay mare.

He clenched his teeth and grabbed his hat from the ground, then craned his neck to look far into the sky. "Why, God? Why are You doing this to me? You got something against me?"

He slapped on his hat, rolled up his bed, strapped on his guns, and picked up his saddle. Taking off on foot, he went in search of his missing horse. He noticed among the boot prints the hoof marks were unclear—like those of a horse running—but the tracks headed east, back the way he'd come. And none marred the way west. It figured.

As he covered the rough ground, Penny's words returned to haunt him. No one had ever given him any "good thing," least of all God. Derek had fought for every morsel of a good thing he'd owned. Why should Penny think the Almighty God would actually do something nice for him, when his own father hadn't cared enough to show a kindness in the past twenty-four years while he'd been alive? And for a lot of that time, he hadn't been visible to Derek, either. Why should he trust God at all?

He died so that you could live.

The words from her reading and the following discussion with her girls whispered through his mind.

"Why would he do that, Mama?" he remembered Olivia asking, tears in her eyes. *"His death sounds so painful. Worse even than being tarred and feathered. Like Grandda talked about in his story of what happened to that man in Boston."*

"Jesus' death was far more painful. He went through it because He loves us. He wanted us with Him. Like family."

Family.

Brooding, Derek looked at the rose-colored sun. He'd been given the opportunity to reunite with his family on more than one occasion but had lost the chance then. Had lost it now. His ma was never coming back, and he'd ruined any possibility of reconciling with Clay. As for Linda. . . now that the shock of his pa's indiscretion had passed, he acknowledged the truth of their kinship, despite what he'd said. He wondered about the woman, who looked younger than the nineteen years she'd claimed. Her bravado was as ill fitted as her gown, and he wondered for the first time if it were all a ruse. Now that he recalled, she had seemed a mite too anxious, jumping at every sudden noise. But any chance of trying to get to know his half sister he'd likely shot full of holes with his harsh treatment of her.

Derek's thoughts traveled to his legacy and the outlaws from the previous morning. His jaw hardened, and he tried to recall if he'd seen them in Silverton. Was it just happenstance that they traveled along this river and the path to the mine at this time, or was his pa's secret map not so secret after all? His pa had always been a braggart. Maybe those outlaws had heard about the silver that Michael Burke had uncovered and aimed to try to steal the claim right out from under Derek's nose. Just as they'd stolen his horse.

They had to have stolen his horse.

And they would live to regret it.

ta

With grim resolution, Penny fed her girls breakfast, fielding their questions about Derek's absence with carefully chosen words. "He had something he needed to take care of. He won't be coming back."

"You mean he just left us?" Christa hugged her doll tighter, tears glistening in her eyes.

"He wouldn't do that," Olivia assured her sister, then turned to Penny. "Would he, Mama?"

"Sometimes a man is given little choice. Olivia, would you like to pick the reading today?" Penny said, changing the subject, her words overbright. "I'll even let you read."

The coveted honor didn't make her daughter's eyes sparkle as Penny had hoped.

While Olivia stumbled over an account they'd previously read—of a man who'd received mercy for an enormous debt, who then refused to forgive another man who owed him a pittance in comparison and was delivered to his tormenters—Penny felt a measure of the same discomfort that had struck her the night before. The girls were silent once Olivia closed the book.

Christa's expression grew even more solemn. "Does that mean we gotta forgive them evil miners, Mama?"

Penny sought for an answer concerning the other subject she would have preferred to avoid.

"I did." Olivia's quiet admission stunned Penny. "I was mad when they took our laying hen and we didn't have any more eggs. But I knew I had to do it."

"You did?" Penny asked.

Olivia nodded. "The words didn't come easy, but I remembered Pa telling me that the hard things never are. We talked about forgiveness the week before he got bit. I was mad at somethin' Christa done, and he said I had to forgive her or I'd never rest easy. So I told God I forgave them miners during my prayers before bed. Did you feel any different when you forgave 'em, Mama?"

Choked, Penny turned away. "We have to get these things packed up. Olivia, I need your help to hitch the team to the wagon."

"We're going west without Mr. Burke?" Christa asked.

"Not west. East."

Both girls stopped gathering the utensils and stared at Penny.

"We're going home."

"Yippee!" Christa's smile lit up the glum morning, and she clapped her hands as best she could with the spoons in them, clinking them together.

"Really, Mama?" The sparkle that had been absent now shone in Olivia's eyes. "Back to our valley?"

Penny regarded them in confusion. "You want to go back there? Those miners are still somewhere around, and I can't see them leaving any time soon. They can still make trouble for us."

"Yeah, but there we have the stream to fish in!"

"And our valley with all the pretty wildflowers," Christa added.

"And the wee butterflies to chase!"

"Aye, that we do." Penny shook her head in amazement that her girls had never wanted to leave. "I suppose your mother has even learned a lesson from all this."

"What's that, Mama?" Christa cocked her head, as though surprised to hear that her elders never stopped learning.

"Troubles find us no matter where we go. Running doesn't solve a thing, and I'm thinkin' if we are again forced to fight, it might be easier to do so when we're in home territory and secure in our surroundings."

Christa smiled. "You miss our valley, too, Mama?"

Penny came to terms with what she'd been denying ever since she left. "Aye, I miss it. But never you mind now. We need to stop this foolish bit of reminiscing and start this day. I want to cover as many miles as we can travel."

"I'll tend to the horses!"

"I'll help Livvie!"

Penny watched her girls, secure again in their happiness, scurry to the area where the black mare and stallion were tethered.

She, too, had something that must be tended and didn't wish to put it off another moment now that she'd made the difficult decision. Facing the birth of the sunrise over the hills, she stared at the misty veils of rose, blue, and violet. Veils that opened the day and announced the glorious approach of the sun.

The words to forgive didn't come easy, as Olivia had warned. But the desire to release the wearisome burden pushed them to the surface. Once her prayer was complete, Penny smiled, at last sensing her Father's approval.

❧

Derek continued his trek eastward, his anger at the outlaws mounting with each stumble he took. To steal his horse, they would have had to come across Penny's camp before they had reached Derek. Worry dueled with rage, each trying to find a target in his mind.

He'd been a fool to leave.

They'd been fools to try him.

"If they hurt her or those sweet girls, so help me. . ."

His muttered threat went unfinished. Up ahead, partially shielded by a tall patch of greasewood, his bay stood, calm as could be, as though Derek hadn't spent the past mile or more walking.

"I don't believe it." Derek gaped at the sight before approaching his mare, slow and easy. A quick appraisal assured him she was all right, and a second one showed him the tether he'd tied to the branches last night was frayed at the bottom.

His jittery mare must have shied at something while he slept, and the worn leather had broken loose. He'd been so weary he could have slept through an earthquake. But instead of being a horse that was faithful to its master by returning or at least remaining in the near vicinity, his mare had decided to lead him on a merry chase.

"Why do I put up with you, horse?"

His beast whinnied, giving a little toss of her head.

He'd never named his horse like some men did their animals. He hadn't planned to keep her after he'd first bought her three years ago and discovered her quirk of shying at every blessed thing. Her reputation foiled every attempt to sell her.

"Maybe you have more courage than I gave you credit for," he mused. "You knew we shouldn't leave Penny on her own. So you headed back, even if I didn't have the sense God gave a mule to do the same."

The horse whickered, her muzzle finding rest in Derek's palm.

"Sorry. A horse." Relief to find his bay made him calm some. "Maybe you do deserve a name."

In no time, he saddled his runaway mare and continued east.

The memory of how it felt to think someone stole his goods while he'd been sleeping brought back the guilt that had dogged him ever since he crept past his slumbering brother and half sister to take their maps. If he hadn't known deep in his gut that it was wrong, he wouldn't have been so secretive about the whole thing. And he didn't wish on anyone the horrible, gut-wrenching feeling of waking up to find his valuables missing.

Valuable. First time he'd ever considered his horse valuable. He supposed he could even consider her a blessing—that is, when she didn't shy and run away. He had bought her at a fair price, and they'd shared numerous days together, traveling the countryside. But she didn't talk back, and he found he missed hearing another human voice. Penny's voice wishing him good morning. The girls' smiles and laughter. Even their never-ending chatter he'd eventually grown accustomed to, though they'd stymied him at times with their unexpected questions.

Now the silence of the plains felt deafening and not the least bit comfortable.

Penny and her girls were a "good thing"; he would even go so far as to call them blessings. Most of the time. But what if. . .what if God did have a hand in Derek's life? What if He aimed to give Derek a family and would rather he no longer remained a lone drifter? And what if Penny and her girls were that family? They'd been thrown together by chance—or had it been more? No matter that Derek had gotten away—twice—he always found himself drawn back to her. Desired to be with her. Even now. Especially now.

He loved her.

"What have I gone and gotten myself into this time?" he muttered, but his heart confirmed his thoughts. He couldn't imagine living the rest of his life without Penny Crawder by his side. Could he convince her to take another chance on him? Would she be willing to listen if he tried to talk to her again?

As he rode on, her teachings to her girls about God, about His desire for His children's happiness, about so many things revolved inside Derek's mind until he couldn't take any more and he bowed his head, yielding to the strong tug at his heart. Despite the blazing sun, he took off his hat and held it over his chest.

"I was wrong to steal from my kin. I admit it. I think I was wrong about You, too, Lord. Ma said You forgive men, and I sure could use a dose. I've messed things up pretty badly. But if You're willing to take a chance on me, I'd be grateful."

The curious ease that filled him, like floating atop saltwater, dissolved when in the early evening he reached the last place they had camped. Only the remains of a dead fire and the ruts from wagon wheels marked that they'd ever been there. He peered over the land to the east, hoping to catch sight of her wagon in the distance. But that was too much to hope for, he supposed, since she likely left after dawn. He had assumed he would meet Penny on the journey back, but she must have turned around, now that she realized the trail was too dangerous for Christa. That meant she was headed back to the canyon and might come across those outlaws a second time.

Six guns or not, Derek didn't rest easy at the idea of her meeting up with them again. And he had the troubling sensation that something wasn't right.

He prodded his mare to a faster pace. "Sorry, horse, I know you're tired." And for the second time, he uttered a prayer. "Please, God, keep Penny and the girls safe."

By the time he neared the canyon, nighttime had wrapped the land in a shroud of darkness. He was grateful for the moon, though he still didn't see the wagon. Penny had covered more miles than usual, clearly eager to get home. He urged his horse forward, between hills.

At the glow of a campfire, his heart beat a little faster, and when he made out the pale canvas of the wagon's tarpaulin, he drew a breath in relief.

A breath that died when he entered camp and saw no one there.

"Penny?" He rode closer to the back of the wagon. "You in there?"

When no answer came, he edged back the cover to peek inside.

Empty.

Alarmed, he scanned the area. Something pale and out of place caught his eye near a clump of sagebrush by the river. He rode closer and dismounted to pick up what looked like twined husks covered by a strip of calico. He turned it over.

His heart lunged as he stared down at Christa's doll.

thirteen

"Mama, I'm scared."

Her arms around a wooly gray coyote pup, Christa retreated a step, almost losing balance as another pup frisked at her heels. In front and around her a coyote pack moved in, slow and dangerous. Teeth bared. Growling low in their throats. Their long bushy tails stuck out behind them in clear threat.

"Don't move, Christa. Don't be scared. And don't put down that pup."

Penny had scarcely known such terror as she did standing several yards behind the pack and watching the three ferocious beasts bear down on her tiny daughter. She sighted her shotgun on the lead dog's head, targeting the scruffy white area behind its pointed ears. Two shots. She had two shots in the dark against three angry coyotes.

"Livvie," she said in a hushed tone to her eldest, who stood quiet and trembling beside her, slingshot poised. "Don't use that. Not yet. If you miss, you'll make them angrier, and they could turn on you. As long as Christa keeps holding that pup, I think she's safe. No mama is going to attack and risk her pups getting hurt."

At least she hoped not. Again a fervent prayer for divine protection rose to her lips. She silently issued the brief plea and kept the shotgun ready in her hands now slick with sweat.

"Livvie, hurry back to camp and fetch a branch from the fire!"

Penny jerked her head around, shocked to hear Derek's whisper behind her. She'd been so focused on her daughter and the growling beasts she hadn't heard his approach.

Sitting on horseback, his eyes on Christa, he raised his pistol into the air and shot. At the explosions that echoed off the canyon walls, the coyotes jumped in their looming semicircle, clearly startled, but didn't scatter. The two biggest dogs turned halfway around and snarled at Derek.

Penny watched as Olivia came running back with a torch and handed it up to him. He rode closer to Christa, thrusting the fire at the nearest coyote. Penny's heart nearly stopped to see how close his hand came to the beast's sharp teeth. Growling and barking, the pack backed away from both Derek and Christa. One of the dogs suddenly jerked and yipped as a rock hit its long snout. Penny swung her gaze to Olivia, who stood poised with her slingshot. The coyote ran off.

"Christa, put the pup down, slowly," Penny called. While her tiny daughter did as instructed, Penny followed Derek's lead and fired a shot into the air. The female coyote grabbed her pup by the scruff and raced away. The second pup scampered after her at a slower pace and disappeared from sight. The remaining coyote, which Penny assumed was the male lead dog, glared at Penny and growled. Its eyes glowed a menacing yellow in the fire from Derek's torch. Penny backed up and stumbled. The huge, lean beast moved her way.

Olivia let loose with a volley of rocks and another shot exploded from Derek's gun. The lead dog yipped and Penny saw dark blotch its gray coat as it turned, racing after its pack.

❧

The coyotes gone, Derek threw his torch to the ground and grabbed Christa, swinging her atop his horse. He had struggled to control his mare and was shocked his beast hadn't shied as he fought off the coyote pack. Penny ran and met him halfway, holding her arms up for her daughter. Derek gently lowered Christa into her embrace, and watched Penny hug her child close.

"How many times have I told you not to wander off?" she chided, kissing the top of her head.

"I'm sorry, Mama." Christa's voice trembled. "I had to go tend nature's call, and I saw the pups and followed them. They wanted to play. Then them big ole mean dogs came."

"Promise me you'll never do something so foolish again, Christa."

She nodded, solemn. "I promise."

"Thank you," Penny mouthed to Derek, and he gave a short nod.

"We should head back to camp and put more distance between us and them," he said quietly, his heart tugging at the picture they made. "Their den must be near. Them pups are too young to go far from it, and where you camped is too close for my peace of mind."

Penny nodded, asking no questions. In the shock of all that had happened, she seemed to take his return to them for granted.

Once back at the campsite, she gave quiet orders for Christa to get inside the wagon and stay there and for Olivia to help hitch up the team. Instead of joining her, however, Penny only stared into the fire, hugging herself as if in a stupor.

"I told the girls, just this morning, that we can't escape from troubles," she said, "that they always have a way of finding us. But I had no idea I'd be fightin' a pack of angry coyotes to top off the day." Her shoulders trembled as she took a deep breath.

"I bedded down early and awoke to find Christa gone. I was terrified to find her with that pup and the pack closing in."

Derek moved to stand beside her and laid his hand on her shoulder. He understood. His own heart had chilled at the sight. And later, his fear had soared when he'd seen the lead dog stalk Penny.

"I'm all right," she assured, but her smile faltered, her eyes still holding a hint of the terrible panic she must have suffered.

"No. You're not pulling away this time," he whispered and drew her to him before she could resist. "Lean on me, Penny. I'm here. And I'm not going anywhere."

Once his arms closed around her trembling body, she melted against him, soft and warm. He held her for some time, his hand smoothing her silken hair, while around them, insects buzzed, and nearby, the fire crackled low. The night again grew still and at peace.

Her shaking subsided, and she pulled away to look into his eyes. "I never thought I'd see you again. Why did you return, Derek? Did you read your pa's map wrong and lose your way?"

He deserved that. Her gentle words held no bite; still they stung. "I came to tell you I was wrong. And to ask that you come back with me to Silverton."

"Come back with you?"

He nodded, unsure now how she would respond to his next request. "While I was heading back here, I made my peace with God. And I want to try and set things right with my family if it's not too late."

"Family?" Her eyes had begun to sparkle, her smile growing throughout his explanation. She raised her brow, urging him to speak the words.

"Yeah, family. My brother. And my sister."

"I can't tell you how pleased I am with your decision," she said, her words cautious. "And I feel so wretched for the shameful way I acted earlier. I was wrong, too, to lash out the way I did."

"Don't give it another thought. Fact is, your words helped set me on this course."

"Then I'm glad, though I still wish I would have dealt with the matter differently. It's the right thing to do, Derek, no matter how difficult. I'm not sure how I can help, being nothing but a stranger to them, but aye, I'll come with you. After all you've done for me and mine, how can I refuse?"

A bit nervous, he pulled his lips into a pucker and rolled his tongue along the inside of his cheek. "Well, it's more than that really. Fact is, my heart hasn't been quite right since I met you."

She paused. "Maybe I can find a cure for you among my cuttings."

"Well, no. That's not exactly what I meant, either."

"Then tell me, Derek. What is on your mind?" She thought she knew but wanted him to say it.

"I love you," he said simply. "I'm tired of being a loner, and I want you to spend the rest of your days with me."

Even though she'd hoped for it, his straightforward answer nearly took her breath away.

"Marry me, Penny." His hands gently clasped her arms. "Come back with me to Silverton. There must be someone there who can tell us where to find a man of the cloth to perform the ceremony."

"Aye, Derek."

His brow shot up at her swift answer. "You'll marry me?"

"Of course."

"You don't need time to think it over?" From what little he'd heard from an old acquaintance, women always asked for time to reach that decision.

"I've thought of little else. I've hoped for this almost since the day I met you. Could you not be tellin'? 'Tis not any drifter I allow the favor of a kiss."

Baffled, he shook his head at her teasing words and returned her smile. "You've known that long?"

"Aye."

"So you're telling me I never had a chance?"

She laughed. "Of course you had a chance. We must make our own choices, Derek. I just hoped you would come to see that marrying me was the right one for you."

He chuckled at her logic. How he longed to pull her into his arms and kiss her! But he held back as Olivia walked into view, and he recalled their need to break camp. He doubted the coyote pack would return to their den soon, if they returned at all, but he didn't want to take that chance.

Unable to resist Penny's appeal, he did kiss her smooth brow. "We won't go far, just enough to put some distance between us and them coyotes." He glanced at Olivia, who brought the horses around. "Should we tell the girls about us?"

"Maybe it's best to wait till morning. I don't want them whooping and hollerin' and alerting every wild beast in the area to our presence."

"Coyotes tend to shy from loud noises. I've had a run-in with their kind before."

She grinned. "Well then, maybe we should tell the girls now, so as to keep the coyotes away."

He laughed; she had the gift for bringing that out in him. "Are you sure Olivia or Christa won't mind having me for a pa?"

"Judgin' by how miserable they behaved after you left,

I think they'll be so excited they won't sleep for days."

He drew her to his side. "Thank God you're safe, Penny, and that I got here in time."

"Aye. I have a great deal for which I need to be thankin' Him." She looked up at Derek, a light in her eyes he'd never before seen. "I had thought that to take my girls and find a better life in Carson City was God's will, as well as my own, even though I faltered with misgivings. Now I realize what must have been His true intent—that I find and become acquainted with you. And I feel peace in that knowledge, that this has been His will from the start. Where we live doesn't matter as long as I'm with you, Derek. I love you, too. I think I must have for some time."

This time, he didn't resist as he leaned down and touched his lips to her soft ones in a slow, tender kiss; one she returned in full.

Afterward, they both noticed Olivia had broken from her task of hitching the harness to the team and stared at them, her mouth agape. Her lips turned up until they stretched into a jubilant smile. Christa also peeked from behind the canvas at the back of the wagon, grinning wide, then covered her mouth and giggled when Derek caught sight of her.

"Well, if they didn't know before, they know now," he whispered, and Penny laughed.

"Olivia, Christa," she said, "before we leave here, we have something to tell you. . . ."

Derek and Penny shared a glance and a smile, before he took her hand in his and they walked closer to share their news with her girls. . .soon to be his girls, too.

Penny had been right. Their whoops and hollers filled the canyon, enough to scare any coyote away.

fourteen

Both eager and anxious, Penny once more donned her mother's native wedding dress and necklace of glass beads. She had been given the room Derek's half sister, Linda, once used, and which she and her girls now shared. Upon their arrival to Silverton more than a week before, they had learned that Linda vanished the morning after Derek left, without a word to anyone. Only the man at the livery remembered her hitching a ride on a miner's wagon leaving town, and Penny had seen both regret and concern in Derek's eyes when he heard the news.

"We'll find her, if that's what you're wantin'," she'd assured him softly.

"I'm not sure I have the right or even that she'll welcome my concern. Clay sure hasn't forgiven me."

Regardless, Derek searched, but found no trace of his half sister.

Penny mused over her initial meeting with her soon-to-be brother-in-law, Clayton, who favored Derek and possessed the same lean strength, and quiet, often brooding manner. He'd treated news of their engagement with shock, and addressed Penny with a shy, almost boyish respect. To her surprise, others in the small town had been polite to her as well, though she received suspicious, even bitter looks from some. With Derek near and her own experience using a gun, Penny felt assured she and her girls would be safe.

Yet while Clay had been kind to her and her girls, he barely spoke to his brother. That first day he'd accepted his portion of the map from Derek, but not the apology, leaving the small parlor area before Derek could finish.

Penny sighed. So much hurt. So many wounds to heal.

All week, she had played mediator between brothers, trying to exhibit both patience and understanding as her da and grandfather had done when they acted as go-betweens for the settlers and natives. This war between brothers was far different, and she hoped less brutal. At least she witnessed Derek make the effort to offer peace on more than one occasion. Gently, she'd advised him not to stir up more strife and to let God work with Clay, and Derek agreed.

She ran her fingertips over the yellow and blue border she'd stitched in the deerskin over her heart, using the last of her precious glass beads to symbolize the sun and the Son, who'd led Penny and Derek through the wilderness. God had played such an important part in their tattered lives, and she knew that He would always be at the core of their marriage. He had brought them together and ordered their steps. When their foolishness had torn them apart, His Spirit whispered to both their hearts, mending each with bright love and mercy and bringing them together once more, soon to be as one.

They had talked over their future, and decided to live in her beautiful valley but not in the shanty Oliver had built. Instead, Derek would build them a home on the other side, at the end of the stream. He planned to start a ranch with his share of the profits from the silver, and when he'd told her what their future would involve, she felt eager to begin life as a cattle rancher's wife. "But first," he'd told her gently, "we have to find the mine."

She didn't mind. As long as she was with him, anywhere was home.

"Penny, are you in there?"

Clay's voice coming from beyond the muslin that covered the entrance jarred her thoughts to the present. She moved forward to pull the weighted cloth back.

He'd shaven off his thick growth of whiskers, and his shoulder-length curls still hung damp. "You look nice," he said, seeming uncomfortable. "You sure you want to go through with this?"

"Completely."

"You could do better." With the way she stared in shock, his face flushed. "No, I don't mean me. Like as not, I'll never marry. But any man would be better than my brother."

"You don't really mean that," she chided softly, and he lowered his eyes. "Clay, I know there's been a lot of hurtful things said and done between you both, but trust me when I say Derek has come to a full understanding of his mistakes. He wants to be makin' amends and doin' right by his family."

Clay scoffed. "Tell that to Linda, if you can find her." He shuffled his boots as though ashamed of his outburst. "I know you mean well, Penny. If it weren't for you and that you asked me to come, I wouldn't even be here today."

"Thank you for that." She laid a hand on his sleeve, already feeling a strong sisterly kinship for this young man, seven years her junior. She hoped he would one day find the happiness that she and Derek had found. Like Derek had once done, Clay, too, was running from God.

"I came to tell you the preacher's arrived," he said. "Derek had to ride outside town to some miner's camp to find him. He was delivering last rites. Kind of a fitting mood for the day."

"Clayton," she quietly chided. "Please don't do this."

At her steady look, he sighed with a sort of weary resignation. "Sorry."

"I love him. I want to be his wife. I'm happy to marry him."

He shook his head as if he couldn't understand her. Nothing Clay said caused her to hesitate or regret her decision. Throughout these past weeks, she'd seen the bitter conflict silently rage inside Derek—but a burning sincerity in his eyes had replaced it, along with his fervent desire to do right. Given time, Clay would see that his brother had changed.

"Mama, Mama!" Christa burst into the small room, her face aglow with excitement. She looked a good deal improved, and it was no secret she'd ferreted a soft spot in a couple of the gruff men's hearts—men who'd lost family, like the hotel manager, who'd become protective of Penny's small girls. She'd warned both never to go near the saloons, but she knew her girls had their own watchmen to ensure they stayed safe, as well as Derek, and their soon-to-be uncle Clay.

"Lookit what I found!" Thrusting a bunch of blue and white posies upward, Christa almost hit Penny in the nose with them. "Livvie says brides are s'pposed to have bouquets, and I made one for you."

"Thank you, Christa." Penny took them in delight and inhaled the sweet fragrance mingled with earth and sun. "They're beautiful."

"Just like you, Mama." Christa grinned from ear to ear.

Olivia trailed in, blowing out a few high notes on her grandda's harmonica. Derek had spent hours instructing her, and Olivia rarely went anywhere without it. She stopped and grinned, lowering the instrument at the sight of Penny. "Mr. Burke is gonna flat keel over when he gets sight of you."

"I hope that's not the case." She smiled at her two

daughters, their own hair shining and freshly braided, their faces rosy. "I declare, it isn't often I see my two girls looking so clean. And Olivia, don't you think after today you should call him something other than Mr. Burke?"

She cocked her head, seeming to consider. "You think he'd mind if I call him Pa?"

"I'll see you in the parlor," Clay murmured and left the crowded room before Penny could acknowledge him.

"Aye, I think he'll like that," Penny answered her daughter.

Olivia regarded her with uncertainty. "You think our real papa would mind?"

Christa's expression also grew anxious.

"No." Penny drew her small daughters close and held them. She thought she understood; they had come to love Derek and wanted him for a pa, but they didn't want to betray their real father by accepting a new one. "I think he'd agree 'tis a fine thing. And it's perfectly all right for you always to keep that special place in your heart meant just for him. There's room enough in those big hearts of yours for two papas, don't you think?"

Olivia smiled and nodded.

"Do you think he's watching us from heaven?" Christa whispered, peering up at the wooden beams.

"Well now, I don't know about that. But if he can and is, I'm sure he's looking down on his two girls with a great deal of approval. He'd be pleased to know we're content and going on with our lives. That was the kind of man he was; he wanted everyone happy." And that was the one reason why Penny finally had been able to release her pain of losing him; she knew Oliver would prefer that she not mourn his absence but would want instead that she open her heart to find love again.

She took a deep breath, preparing for the next step, and smiled. "And are you both ready to be joinin' me in this bonnie new adventuresome life that will be ours?"

"Aye!" Olivia said without hesitation, and Christa giggled, clapping her hands.

Minutes later, with one of her daughters on each side of her escorting her, Penny made her way into the cramped parlor area where Derek, Clay, and the minister waited.

"Hello, Mr. Matthis," Christa said in a loud voice to the man standing across the room near Clay. "I didn't know you were coming." Penny shushed her daughter, and the elderly hotel manager winked at Christa in greeting.

Then Penny saw Derek.

Her breath stalled as he turned from speaking with the preacher to face her, and she paused a moment to take in the change.

Clean-shaven, with his long, wavy hair trimmed and slicked back, he made a striking figure. A clean shirt of deep blue accented his eyes, and the black string tie he wore at his collar made him look like the gentleman she knew him to be. She'd rarely seen him minus his hat or without his hair hanging in his face and appreciated his fine, strong features, amazed at how handsome he really was.

As she walked forward, holding Christa's bouquet, and took her place beside him, his admiring gaze showed her he also approved of her choice. Derek touched the few wildflowers Penny had woven into one of her braids at her temple and smiled.

"My Penny." His words came quiet so only she could hear, but they echoed to the very core of her heart, creating a warm glow.

Behind them, Olivia began to play the harmonica. Stunned, Penny glanced her way, recognizing the tune as an old Scottish love song her da had once played, one of her favorites. She looked back at Derek in question.

He shook his head. "I taught her other songs and gave advice. She picked out the notes to that one from what she remembered your da teaching her. She thought it would make you happy and asked if she could play it today. I hope you approve."

"Aye." Tears misted Penny's eyes, and she felt, while listening to the sweet, lilting music, as if a part of her da were there with them. In his granddaughters, his legacy and her mother's legacy would never die. She would see to that.

She laid her hand in Derek's, hoping that with her eyes she expressed all the love she felt for him. With Derek, she would start a similar but new legacy.

A legacy of love and hope and faith that would carry on throughout the generations.

A Letter To Our Readers

Dear Reader:

In order that we might better contribute to your reading enjoyment, we would appreciate your taking a few minutes to respond to the following questions. We welcome your comments and read each form and letter we receive. When completed, please return to the following:

Fiction Editor
Heartsong Presents
PO Box 719
Uhrichsville, Ohio 44683

1. Did you enjoy reading *A Treasure Reborn* by Pamela Griffin?
   ❑ Very much! I would like to see more books by this author!
   ❑ Moderately. I would have enjoyed it more if

   _____

   _____

   _____

2. Are you a member of **Heartsong Presents**? ❑ Yes ❑ No
   If no, where did you purchase this book? _____

   _____

3. How would you rate, on a scale from 1 (poor) to 5 (superior), the cover design? _____

4. On a scale from 1 (poor) to 10 (superior), please rate the following elements.

   ____ Heroine   ____ Plot
   ____ Hero   ____ Inspirational theme
   ____ Setting   ____ Secondary characters

5. These characters were special because? _____
   _____
   _____

6. How has this book inspired your life? _____
   _____
   _____

7. What settings would you like to see covered in future
   Heartsong Presents books? _____
   _____
   _____

8. What are some inspirational themes you would like to see
   treated in future books? _____
   _____
   _____

9. Would you be interested in reading other **Heartsong
   Presents** titles?   ❏ Yes   ❏ No

10. Please check your age range:
    ❏ Under 18   ❏ 18-24
    ❏ 25-34   ❏ 35-45
    ❏ 46-55   ❏ Over 55

Name _____
Occupation _____
Address _____
City, State, Zip _____

Heart♥ng

HEARTSONG PRESENTS TITLES AVAILABLE NOW:

(If ordering from this page, please remember to include it with the order form.)

Presents

Great Inspirational Romance at a Great Price!

Heartsong Presents books are inspirational romances in contemporary and historical settings, designed to give you an enjoyable, spirit-lifting reading experience. You can choose wonderfully written titles from some of today's best authors like Wanda E. Brunstetter, Mary Connealy, Susan Page Davis, Cathy Marie Hake, Joyce Livingston, and many others.

When ordering quantities less than twelve, above titles are $2.97 each.
Not all titles may be available at time of order.